IN EXCHANGE

AN URBAN THRILLER

K.L. HALL

B. LOVE PUBLICATIONS

SYNOPSIS

When the love of my life is the bad boy instead of the prince...
It was a simple arrangement.
People desperate for a come-up for different reasons.
It wasn't supposed to snowball into real feelings or a fairytale proposal.
And definitely *not* a surprise pregnancy.
To most, my fiancé, Kareem Solomon, is the self-proclaimed, privileged prince of NOLA with a radiant smile and a heart of gold.
His family's deep pockets have managed to hide his missteps.
A year ago, I was hired to help save him from his demons, reel him in from his depression, and rebuild the man his best friend and family once knew and loved.
In exchange, I would get the payout of my dreams and everything I needed to open my restaurant.
The catch? It's his best friend who makes my pulse skitter.
Psalm Baptiste is everything I've ever wanted: handsome, poised, and an arrogant demeanor that leaves me dazzled.
Born and bred in the bayou, he wields the power and money to dismantle or rescue my heart.
I didn't know what our agreement would mean for us.

That I would be spellbound by the number of zeros on the check *and* the essence of him.

That signing my name on the dotted line would leave three hearts hanging in a gray area.

That I would become the villain of my own love story.

It's only a matter of time before the truth comes out and everything implodes.

But until then…

This steamy novella was previously titled House of Cards.

"Don't fuck no bitch that's fuckin' with yo' dawg, that's law."
-Yo Gotti

Trigger Warning:

The theme of this story is love and how far you'll go in the name of it for the ones you love, the ones you care about the most. Not every character is afforded the luxury of a traditional "happily ever after." This book contains instances and/or mentions of violence, suicide, abuse, and explicit language. Reader discretion is advised.

WARNING!

*Before you turn (or swipe) this page, please be aware of the potential side
effects of an urban thriller penned by K.L. Hall:*
Anxiety, insomnia due to excessive reading, heart palpitations, or a
calming feeling accompanied by a tingling sensation between your
thighs. Please contact your literary professional if you experience any of
these side effects by leaving a five-star review once you've recovered.
Last, for your safety while reading this story, please keep both hands on
your Kindle device at all times and enjoy the ride.

PROLOGUE

Only Fools Fall in Love *for Free*

Lotus Pierce

There are two kinds of people in the world: those who will do anything to survive and those who won't. After my mama kicked me out at seventeen for refusing to acknowledge her weird-ass new husband as my stepfather, I hit the beaten path of adulthood. Over the next four years, I jumped from one dead-end job *and* couch to another until my cousin Tiffany agreed to put me up in one of her husband's vacant apartments until it was rented. She was four years older than me, and although she was married to a real estate agent with connections, she *always* had a baller on speed dial. I looked up to her for two reasons: her beauty and her hustle. With a safe and free place to lay my head, I continued scraping pennies to save up for my restaurant. It was my dream to become an upscale restaurant owner. *Lotus* would be the finest restaurant in the French Quarter, selling Cajun and French Creole cuisine. Opening *Lotus* was a dream I shared with my late father, who died of a heart attack when I was fourteen. All I ate for breakfast, lunch, and dinner was Ramen noodles to make sure our dream became a reality. Being broke did two things for me: it shortened my tolerance for bullshit and reinforced my ambition.

My downtrodden narrative changed when Tiff mentioned an online ad she'd seen looking for young, beautiful women interested in making cash daily with no experience necessary. She told me I had the type of face that could bring in millions and that with her guidance and a small kickback to her for looking out, I could be on the fast track to getting my restaurant. Her motto: *only fools fall in love for free.* Back then, I didn't know how right she was. Still, it sounded too easy to be legit and too damn good to be true. But, I trusted her, so I called the number listed at the bottom of the ad anyway. My ass was hungry for a come-up, and Tiff loved money so much, it may as well have been her middle name. Plus, my livelihood depended on having more than a hundred and twenty dollars to my name at any given time.

In the beginning, becoming an escort wasn't all I thought it'd be. Sure, the money was an upgrade from the mediocre pay I was used to, and it helped me stack my money quicker and support myself, but I knew laying on my back and servicing men wasn't something I could do long-term. In my eyes, sex work was another stepping stone I had to use to get me to the next level. And with the way young adulthood had whooped my ass, I was ready for the lavish gifts and international trips I'd seen Tiffany's husband bestow upon her. I felt I deserved it.

In my eyes, Tiff had been on top of the world for as long as I'd known her. Somehow, she'd been lucky enough to figure out the key to life early on and had been basking in happiness ever since. A wave of shame washed over me. I felt bad about hating on my own blood for what she had, especially after she'd looked out for me. But I couldn't help myself. I'd struggled for every sliver of peace I'd ever gotten. Yeah, she'd given me a break by letting me live rent-free, but it was only a matter of time before the other shoe dropped. I had to have a backup plan.

The night a client left me stranded at an upscale holiday soiree in the heart of the French Quarter with *no* money to pay for my drink was when everything changed. When we first arrived, I'd gotten a reading from a tarot card reader hired to entertain guests. She told me she saw wealth, success, and immense heartbreak in my future. At the moment, the only thing I had were empty pockets, so I pushed her reading to the back of my mind.

I sat alone, surrounded by a raw oyster bar, spirited partygoers, and a giant ice sculpture spouting champagne. It was clear I was out of my element, but the authentic double-Cs on my bag made me feel more secure than I did with my knockoffs. I'd spent my last on it. Then my high and mighty ass thought I'd get away with refusing to perform oral sex on my client in the men's room by offering a hand job on the ride home instead. Not only did he get up and leave, but he called the agency I worked for and got my ass fired before his seat turned cold. I was so dumbfounded I couldn't even get up from the cocktail table. *Your ass knows you're going to have to return that bag now.*

Suddenly, I was back at square one, which brought up a lot of negative feelings I had to swallow back down because I was in public. After being an escort for six months, there was no way I could explain the gap in my resume to a nine-to-five employer. Being in a profession where I had to rely on someone else to keep my lights on was no longer it for me. I wanted to be in the driver's seat of my life and *never* have to worry about money again. My thoughts wandered back to my tarot reading. With all the promised wealth in my future, I wanted to know *how* the riches would come and *where* I needed to be to meet the millionaire of my dreams. As many frogs as I'd kissed, I was *ready* for my prince.

My phone vibrated. I looked down to see a text from Tiffany.

"Fuck," I mumbled as I sipped my Long Island Iced Tea slowly, watching it become more watered down as I thought of my next move. She was going to want answers I didn't have to give her. For someone who didn't waste my time making wishes or picking up four-leaf clovers, I spent a lot of time with my head in the clouds and could never seem to come up with a plan that got me long-term money. At the rate I was going, my restaurant would *never* see the light of day. In the midst of my thoughts, someone sat at my table for two.

"Somebody is sitting here," I snapped without even bothering to look at who'd taken a seat to my right.

"How about I make you a deal? If you allow me to sit here, I'll get you a drink," a man with a baritone voice as smooth as butter replied.

Intrigued, I twisted my neck in his direction and almost melted into a puddle of lust right in my seat. The voice was attached to a handsome man with chocolate brown skin, a killer smile, designer clothes from his shoulders down to his size twelve shoes, and *no* ring on his finger.

A girlish grin crept up one side of my mouth before I parted my lips to speak. "And what if I don't want another drink?"

He took a closer look at my glass. "Yeah. It does look like you're babysitting the one you got."

My eyes followed his. "You could pay for this one if you're still interested in keeping that seat," I proposed.

He flashed me a bright grin as a soft chuckle belted past his pouty, brown lips. He wasn't even fully smiling, and looking at him was already like a loaded gun to my chest.

"I'm Psalm, and it's a corporate party, so the drinks are free, by the way," he introduced himself before extending his tattooed right hand.

I blushed with embarrassment before placing my hand in his and shaking it firmly. "Lotus."

"Mmm. Strong handshake."

"Were you expecting something softer?"

His seductive brown eyes snaked along my frame before he spoke. "Not at all."

There was a one-sided pluck of my lips. "Good."

We spent the next few minutes talking. I learned what he did and lied when it came time to discuss my current job status. He was a single, handsome, twenty-six-year-old Chief Financial Officer. And as far as he knew, I was a twenty-two-year-old recent graduate from the University of Chicago interning in NOLA at a start-up tech company. To me, it wasn't serious. We were

two strangers trading stories at a party. Who cared about the truth when telling lies was more entertaining? When things fell silent between us for the first time, I tuned into the buzz of conversation around us.

Psalm leaned in. "Okay, I'll bite. What's up?"

"What do you mean?"

"Why you babysitting that shit? Stiff drinks ain't your thing?"

"Stiff drinks, no. I'm a huge champion of other *stiff* things, though," I quipped.

His soft-looking lips danced around a smile before he sipped his drink. "Noted."

"What are you sippin' on?" I asked curiously.

He kept his eyes stationed on me for a second or two. "Hennessy and Coke."

"Mmm."

"So, you drinkin' with me tonight or nah?"

Instead of responding, I waved down one of the waiters before pushing my drink away. "Hi. I'll have what he's having."

When the party ended, we strolled through the French Quarter, seeing festive decor around every cobblestoned corner. All the buildings were decorated with garland, oversized red bows, and twinkling white lights. He kissed my cheek before calling me an Uber to ensure I got home safely. He didn't ask me to fuck. He didn't try to take advantage of me and take me back to his place. He was a true Southern gentleman, which was something I *rarely* encountered. I never expected to lose my job and embark on a whirlwind romance in the same twenty-four hours, but somehow, I slipped Psalm my number and my heart that night.

In the two months that followed our first encounter, we spent almost every day together. Our connection was so rare and delicate that I didn't share a whiff of him with anyone, selfishly consuming him all for myself. We kissed. We hugged. We made spine-chilling, back-break-ing, sticky, passionate love. I knew I'd never feel for another man what I felt for him. Was it all roses and rainbows? No. When we were together, Psalm had a way of using his polished vocabulary as a way of proving that he was more cultured than I was. It was easily one of my least favorite things about him, but since I was still pretending to be a college graduate, I did my best to match his energy. I was a pro at faking it until I made it. Besides, we all had different versions of ourselves that we promoted, depending on the company we kept. I'd never let him know he used to make me feel like we'd grown up on two separate ends of the world.

The first time he took me to the parish where his childhood home was—a large, four-bedroom in the suburbs with a forest green front door—I realized my feelings were warranted. If I hadn't known I was in New Orleans, I would have sworn we were driving around in one of the uppity neighborhoods on the outskirts of the city I used to pass on the bus on the way to school. If his vocabulary and high-end taste in clothing hadn't already given it away, it was clear he came from more money than I did. Before they died, his parents were published professors and high-paid accountants for Fortune 500 companies. My mother did hair out of our living room six days a week, and I wouldn't have known my father if I had to pick him out in a line-up.

Psalm was a level-up for me in more ways than one. He was poised, direct, and downright sexy. When someone like me found a man who made all the bullshit in my life vanish, it was hard not to feed off his energy. If I couldn't get my finances in order, at least my love life was taking a turn in the right direction. Everything was perfect. And then, he did the worst thing a good man could do to a broken girl. He ghosted me.

I called.

I texted.

I even fucked around and googled him to find his work email.

Nothing.

My mind was stuck in a never-ending cycle of re-living our love story because, by the time I realized we were over, the memories were all I had left. I didn't understand it, nor could I wrap my mind around it. His favorite color was royal blue, the same as mine. He had Greek shaped feet, just like me. He thought pineapples on pizza were a crime against humanity, like me. He poured his milk into the bowl before his cereal like a psycho, just like I did. And he was... gone. I spent a few days trying to settle into the thought that he was dead. It was either that, or he was secretly married. Regardless of the truth, I was shattered. Tiffany was the one who stroked my hair and brought me through my depression when Psalm disappeared. She was the only family member I kept in touch with and the only person I had to lean on in my darkest hour. I spilled everything to her. Something told me she knew the loss I felt, the hollowness left behind when you lose someone you love, but we never talked about it. I was too consumed in my grief to save her from drowning in her own.

A month passed before I got a call from him at two o'clock in the morning. My groggy, sleep-deprived eyes scanned the screen that revealed his name, and my heart sprang forward. He wasn't dead. He was back, and he was calling *me*. As badly as I wanted to send him to voicemail, my heart wouldn't let me draw in my next breath before hearing his voice. I quickly pressed accept and answered with as much attitude as I could muster up in the wee hours of the morning.

"Who is this?" I hissed.

"You know exactly who this is, Lotus."

The sound of my name falling off his tongue made my body quake. "W-what?"

"Before you hang up, let me explain."

I sat up in the bed. "What is there for you to explain? It's clear something or *someone* has had your attention for the past month."

"You're right. I should've called. I should've reached out."

I scoffed. "Yeah. You should've."

"Can you please hear me out?"

"What is there to say? It's been a month, Psalm! An entire *month* without a single word from you. I thought you were dead!"

"Remember my friend Kareem I told you about?"

I sucked my teeth before recalling the name. "What about him?"

"H–he's been going through a lot, and, uh, tried to commit suicide a few weeks ago in the parking garage at his job."

My lashes flipped full-open. He'd sometimes talk about his best friend, Kareem, when recanting stories from his childhood, but our deep conversations were few and far between. I heard the sadness in his voice and immediately felt like a jerk for nosediving off a cliff of conclusions before fully hearing him out.

"I'm so sorry to hear that."

"Yeah. Me too."

"Is he... okay?" I inquired hesitantly.

"No, but he will be. Look, Lotus. I don't know how else to say this, but I need your help."

"My help? Anything. What do you need?"

"I have a proposition for you."

"What is it?"

He blew his lips into the receiver, another indicator of his heightened stress levels. "I don't even know how to put this shit into words that will make sense."

"You can tell me anything, Psalm. Whatever you need from me, I'll do it."

"Do you really mean that?"

I nodded. I'd been so cold without him, and the moment he returned, it was as if everything in me began to thaw, and I could feel again. He was back in my life, and I was ready to move mountains to keep him around. "I do."

He sighed. "Listen, I-I've been worried about him. Me, his mom, and his dad, we've all been. He needs help, and it's not the kind of help *we* can give him. And it's fucked up because he's a great guy. He's intelligent and loyal as hell. He's crazy skilled at playing the piano, too. Like, really fuckin' good. But he's been treated for borderline personality disorder since he's been back. That, coupled with his PTSD, has made it hard for him to readjust socially."

"*Back*? Where was he?"

"In the Army stationed overseas," he answered.

"Psalm, what is your proposition?" I quizzed softly.

"I want to set you up with him."

My forehead creased in confusion, and I recoiled as if he and his request physically repelled me. "Wait. What?"

Not only did my heart belong *only* to him, but I had zero interest in getting to know Kareem, no matter how heart-wrenching his story was. Psalm was the man I wanted, and after everything we'd shared, I couldn't understand why he didn't see that too.

"I know what I'm asking you to do is crazy, but we don't know what else to do. Watching someone you love become a ghost is... it's just hard to do, y'know?"

"You damn right, it's crazy! Love doesn't make a mental illness go away. There I was, thinking you were about to ask me to do something to help *you*. Do you not know how I feel about you?"

"I do."

"Bullshit, because if you did, you would've never asked me that."

"Lotus, I don't know what else to do," he responded, sounding defeated.

My lungs expelled a long huff of air. "Listen, I'm sorry about your friend. I really am. And maybe there's a part of me that respects you for going the extra mile for your nigga, but I want to be *your* girl, Psalm, not his."

"Lotus, I–"

I cut him off. "Was any of it real between us? I know it was fast, but I was falling in love with you, but if all it takes is thirty days for what we had to fade from your mind, you're not the guy I thought you were." The line fell silent for a few seconds, making me question if I was talking to myself. "H-hello?"

"I'm here," he answered.

"Well? What do you have to say? It's been a month, and you still haven't found the words?"

"It was real, Lotus. It was all real, and if this were any other world, I would love you to..."

"But?" I butted in, beating him to the punch before he could say it.

"But blood couldn't make Kareem and me any closer, and if I have to choose between you or him, then I'll *always* love him more."

His words stung like an arrow in my heart. For the first time in history, it seemed the power of friendship was stronger than the power of pussy.

"Well then, I guess there's nothing left to say."

"It's just me and his parents, Lotus. He doesn't have anyone else. He needs a woman to put his pieces back together."

"And what makes you think I can?"

"Because I know you've never stepped foot on UC's campus, let alone graduated from there. I know what you were doing to get money the night I met you sulking at that party, trying to figure out how you were going to pay for a *free* drink."

I shuddered at the reminder, feeling embarrassed all over again. "H-how long have you known?" I stammered, at a loss at what to say back. He'd caught my ass red-handed. I was sweating like a sinner in church.

"My uncle is a tenured professor there. I used his connections and put the pieces together myself. I'm a smart man with a lot of resources at my disposal, Lotus."

I swallowed the melon-sized lump in my throat. "What the fuck does my line of work have anything to do with—"

He cut me off. "How close are you to making your dream a reality?"

My forehead bunched. "What?"

"The restaurant you want to open in the French Quarter," he answered, cutting me off.

"So, you remember that but couldn't remember to call me for a month?"

"What if I told you I could make your dream come true?"

My eyes doubled in size before my brows turned in. "What? How?"

"There's an available space I think might be perfect for your restaurant, and I'll give you the money to buy it."

The ringing of a cash register chimed in my head, perking my ears. As much as I wanted to refuse him off the mere principle of his request, my pockets and my heart were begging for his attention. It wasn't as if I'd landed a six-figure paying job in his absence. I was just as desperate for the money as I was the night we met.

"W-what?"

"Kareem comes from a wealthy family. Between his parents and I, we can give you anything you want *if* you do this."

"What exactly would I have to do?"

"Do whatever you gotta do to make him fall in love with you and see that life is worth living."

I scoffed. "I don't know the first thing about making someone fall in love with me."

"Just do to him what you did when you were with me," he stated.

I paused, biting my lip. Taking the deal meant dancing off into my happily ever after with Psalm would never be in the cards for me. But at least my restaurant would. All I had to do was pretend I had feelings for a basket case with rich parents.

"So, I'm supposed to run off and live happily ever after with him? Because I don't believe in fairytales."

"Good, because that's not what I'm offering."

"How much *are* you offering for my restaurant?"

"One million dollars."

ONE

Empty Wishing Well
Psalm Baptiste
One Year Later.

I parallel parked my polar white S-Class into the vacant parking spot outside Mickey's Pool Hall and killed the engine. My thumb jabbed the lock on the keypad as I smoothed out the loose wrinkles in my white button-up and slightly loosened my navy blue tie. I left my blazer in the car because I was in for a casual pool outing with my boy, Kareem. The smoky hole-in-the-wall was the last establishment I needed to wear my designer loafers in, but when Kareem called, I came running with no questions asked. I stepped onto the dusty sidewalk, making sure to fix my face. I'd already constructed non-triggering compliments and facial expressions to make myself seem relaxed and do anything but assess his mental health on the ride over. If dealing with Kareem's mental issues over the years had taught me anything, it was that the carefree bonds we made as children hardly ever looked the same once we got to adulthood. I guess that was the irony of nostalgia. Those picture-perfect childhood memories would always be frozen in time.

At three years shy of thirty, I'd darted up the corporate ladder and became the youngest CFO of United First Financial Bank, the city's oldest and largest banking institution. Not to mention, I was one of NOLA's most eligible Black bachelors with zero babies or incurable diseases. I pushed my vain thoughts aside the minute I stepped inside and headed straight for the bar.

I waved down the female bartender. "Hennessy and Coke, please."

She returned moments later and placed the rock glass filled with cognac on a white square napkin with her phone number scribbled in purple ink on the corner. I smirked and passed her a fifty-dollar bill for the thirteen-dollar drink.

"Keep the change."

She flashed a smile at me. She was cute, but I never found interest in a woman I didn't have to do a little work to get. If she'd given me her number within the first few minutes of being in my presence, there was no doubt in my mind she'd be willing to bend over at my request. While taking my first swig, I glanced at the flat-screen TV fixated on ESPN. Before I could set the glass back on the bar, a tall, brown-skinned man with a chiseled jawline and a large scar beneath his right eyebrow, and who was in desperate need of a haircut, plopped down beside me.

"What's up, P?" Kareem greeted me before slapping his palm against my shoulder.

"Wassup, bruh? I almost didn't recognize you. All that money you got, and your ass can't afford a forty-dollar haircut?" I asked with a soft chuckle.

I couldn't help but joke on his matted afro. We'd been thick as thieves since we were twelve years old. We'd done almost everything together, from playing on the same football and basketball teams to chasing after the same girls throughout middle and high school. Kareem started showing signs of borderline personality disorder when we were sixteen. He'd always been moody and sensitive in my eyes, but his highs and lows became more apparent. He'd switch from a depressive mood to fits of uncontrolled aggression, wanting to fight everyone in sight.

After graduation was the first time we ventured down different paths since we'd met. I got accepted to NYU and majored in finance with a minor in management and organizations, while Kareem followed in his father's footsteps and enlisted in the U.S. Army straight out of high school. Because of his father's high military status, he was able to have Kareem's private medical records sealed. He had Kareem seen by his hand-picked military doctor, who would ensure Kareem didn't test positive for any banned substances. He served eight years before being honorably discharged. While serving, his convoy was headed into a nearby town when their vehicle took a direct hit from a stray grenade, leaving him as the sole survivor with permanent nerve damage to his left arm, borderline personality disorder, and a shit ton of PTSD. He ended up coming out of the military more fucked up than he was when he went in. Since he'd been back, Kareem had been trying to readjust to civilian life, but the severe conversion didn't come with ease.

"So, what's up, man?" I asked. "You want a beer or something? Order whatever you want. It's on me."

"Everything's cool. Shit, you know me. I'm just living life, taking it one day at a time." He paused, eyes darting over to the bottles behind the bar. "I'll take a Jack Daniels straight up."

I studied him with a frown. "Nigga, since when do you drink Jack Daniels?"

"I'm just trying new shit. Damn, can't I expand my palette?" he quizzed with a soft chuckle.

I shared a short laugh with Kareem before clearing my throat. "No, but for real, man, how you been? How's work? How's life? How's everything?"

We hadn't spoken in a couple of weeks. I'd been tied up in my own business and personal affairs that the most we'd said to one another was sports banter through text about the playoffs.

I watched Kareem frown as his gaze delved deep into the mahogany drink the bartender placed in front of him.

He shook his head. "I told you, everything's fine. I don't feel like talkin' about me right now."

"Then wassup? What you wanna do?"

"I wanna get up and whoop your ass in some pool like the good ol' days," he insisted before pushing himself away from the bar and making his way over to the deserted billiards table in the back corner.

I followed suit and sat my drink on the windowsill before loosening my tie. "Say less. Rack 'em."

———

Hours passed as we played a few games like old times while downing a couple more drinks before Kareem sat at the pub table beside the window. "Yo, Psalm?"

"Yeah?"

"I think my... this mental shit is starting to get the best of me again."

We traded glances before I let my pool stick rest against the table and stepped closer to him. "Your PTSD?" I quizzed, making sure to keep my voice low.

Kareem nodded, and I sat on the bar stool across from him. "Yeah."

"I thought you were taking medicine that kept that under control, man, and what about therapy? Are you still going?"

"I ran out of pills a couple of weeks ago and haven't made another appointment at the VA hospital. Psalm, I-I'm scared, bruh," he confessed.

"Is that why you called me down here?"

Kareem turned away before grazing his hands across his five o'clock shadow. "I thought I could handle it without them. I'm supposed to be tough."

"You are tough, Kareem. You've always been one of the toughest men I know."

"I'm a soldier, Psalm. A fucking soldier! And I can't get through the day without poppin' pills to make me seem normal or at least tolerable. And nobody knows what it's like. Not you, my parents, the people at work, not even... None of y'all know what it feels like to have the blood and brains of your squad members splattered all over you. None of y'all can imagine scrubbing the blood stains of your brothers and sisters, people you *love*, off your American uniform. Can you? Can you imagine that?"

I took a big gulp from my glass, finishing the rest of my drink before responding. I knew I'd need another to maneuver through the conversation ahead of me, but I straightened my posture before sitting on the backless bar stool next to him and listened attentively.

"Tell me what you need, man."

"The pills don't kill the pain no more, Psalm. Nothing does," Kareem admitted.

"What about the therapist you were seeing? When's the last time you spoke to someone about what you're feeling?" Our eyes linked, and before he even opened his mouth to give me an excuse, I sucked my teeth. "You gotta go back to counseling, man, *and* see your doctor. That's what they're there for, to help *you*."

Kareem's head wagged from side to side. "See, this is why I didn't want to bring this shit up in the first place."

"What do you mean?"

"I mean, don't talk to me like I'm broken, nigga. Because I'm not! I can come to terms with a lot of shit, but being broken ain't one of them. If anything, I feel targeted. I'm not trying to use my fucked-up head as a crutch. I don't want to be a burden for the rest of my life!"

"Nobody thinks you're a burden, Kareem."

He kissed his teeth as if to disregard my statement, as if what I said was fake news. "You know, it's been years since I've pumped my own gas because the smell of burning flesh is still embedded in my nose? The flames... the fuel. I-I can't go outside at certain times of the day. Sometimes, I still fuckin' flinch at the sound of loud trucks. I feel like I'm going crazy in my skin, literally watching myself unravel day by day."

His usual, stiffened military posture was hunched over, and he laid his heavy head in his hands as if he were about to start sobbing in the middle of the pool hall.

"Kareem, I–"

He inhaled deeply. "Two nights ago, I jumped out of bed in a cold sweat because I saw the ghost of the fallen soldier who died in my arms the day our convoy got ambushed. His dirt and soot-covered face was as clear as day. Wrong place, wrong time is what I used to tell myself to keep pushing forward... to keep swallowing it all down. I've been back for almost two fuckin' years, and some days, it's like I never left."

"Damn," I muttered with a commiserating tone after listening to my friend's mental and physical setbacks.

I lowered my head, unable to imagine experiencing any of what Kareem had gone through, and to be honest, I didn't want to.

"And the worst part is, I think I'm going to scare Lotus away. She barely lets me touch her. We haven't slept in the same bed in weeks…"

I kept my expression neutral. After years of failed attempts to get Kareem on the right track, mending his internal wounds and battling his demons became something neither his family nor their deep pockets could heal. He needed something or someone to live for. That was why *we* decided to set him up with Lotus. Unfortunately, Kareem had fallen so deep in love with her that he either couldn't or refused to see the writings on the wall. She'd always been in love with someone else, and that someone was me.

"I'm sure you're overreacting. Lotus is a… tough girl," I assured him.

"I know you two don't get along, but—"

"That's putting it mildly. Your girl is a piece of work," I stated matter-of-factly.

"Well, you're gonna have to start getting along with her because I plan on asking her to marry me next weekend," he announced.

His words made me choke on the saliva caught in my throat. "Whoa. Come again," I stated, eyebrows heightened in suspense.

"Yeah, man."

"You sure? It's only been, what, like a year since you started bringing her around?"

"I know it might seem fast, but she came into my life when I needed her the most. I think, nah, I *know* she's the one, Psalm, or the closest thing to it."

I pinned him with a concerned lens while pausing to collect my thoughts. He'd always been methodical, a planner. He never made irrational decisions. It was one thing to look at rings, but to have already selected and purchased one? He was moving at warp speed. *How the fuck could I not have seen this coming?* Kareem's eyes were weary but serious, sure, even. Who was I to talk him out of it?

I cleared my throat before congratulating him. "Yo, congrats," I cheered, raising my glass toward the bartender to bring us another round. I knew alcohol wasn't the best thing after the conversation we'd just had, but the delivery of his news had somehow made him seem lighter. The mere mention of Lotus seemed to put Kareem in better spirits. "This is good news. We gotta toast to this."

He shot me a sliver of a smile. "I never thought I'd see the day, but Lotus is the real deal, bruh."

"Mmm," I grumbled while still trying to keep my eyes from rolling.

He leaned in. "And that's why I need my two favorite people to start getting along and love each other how I love y'all. I can't have my best man and bride-to-be hating each other. A nigga already goin' through enough," he stated with a lighthearted chuckle.

I smiled back before dipping my chin in a nod. "I'll try, man. Anything for you."

I'd never encountered a hurdle I couldn't overcome, or a woman who could resist my wit and charm. If Kareem's happiness depended on me "making amends" with the woman we'd *both* made room for in our hearts, I wouldn't let it happen now.

Kareem shrugged me off with a chuckle. "I've planned it and thought this through. You'll meet her next Saturday at her restaurant. Over dinner, you'll mingle, bury the hatchet, and later that night, I'll show up all decked out with the ring. I'll have the jazz band play something real nice, and then I'll ask her to marry me right there in front of everyone," he explained, sounding giddier than when he told me he kissed Michelle Parker in the sixth grade.

"Seems like you have been giving this a lot of thought," I acknowledged, sipping my new drink.

"I have."

"Then don't worry. I'll handle it all. You just make sure you get a fuckin' haircut before gettin' down on one knee, nigga. It'd be a shame if she turned you down because of this Chia Pet look you got goin' on," I joked.

"Yeah, whatever, nigga. Get up and watch me bust ya ass again," he boasted before grabbing his pool stick.

Two

r. Steal Your Girl
Psalm

The upcoming week flew by, and before I knew it, my eyes cracked open at the sound of my alarm on Saturday morning. I rolled over and felt the warmth of Bianca, my secretary, occupying the usually vacant side of my king-sized bed. I didn't know how she'd managed to negotiate spending the night since it was something I *rarely* permitted. The last woman to wake up in my bed was about to be asked for her hand in marriage by my best friend. Nevertheless, I wagged my head, deciding to bring up the matter later. Before dragging my sluggish limbs out of bed, I shot a glance over my shoulder at Bianca's naked, sleeping body. Her plump, caramel right breast had slipped out from underneath my black Egyptian cotton bedsheets, staring back at me and temporarily derailing my train of thought. My dick pulsed in response, but I ignored the urge.

After scooping up my phone, I headed into the bathroom and closed the door before unlocking the screen. There were unread e-mails about signing financial documents and rearranging upcoming business meetings, all things I felt Bianca should've been handling. She was sexy, but her ass was slipping. Frustrated, I shook my head again and continued to scroll when I came across one from Lotus from the night before with the subject *Tomorrow's Meeting*. I twisted the handle in the shower to let the water warm up before clicking her message and reading it in its entirety.

"Per Kareem's request, I'll meet you at my restaurant tomorrow tonight at eight. Don't be late, Psalm. I don't want to do this anymore than you do."

I could sense her bitterness through the phone, which only made me smile before tapping reply. Without even realizing it, I'd become addicted to her. Lotus was my beautiful disaster. My damsel in distress. The sovereign of my chaos.

My fingers tapped against the screen, delivering my simple response, *"Enjoy your Saturday, Lotus,"* before putting my phone on the bathroom counter and stepping inside the shower.

The steaming water flowed all over me as the words from Lotus's sarcastic e-mail kept replaying in my head. There'd always been something about her that got under my skin. She was the first and only woman ever to have such power over me. From the night we met, we clicked like a gun and bullet. The two months we spent in secrecy together felt so damn good it was sickening. Power naps were her love language, like mine. Her brain was always busy multitasking, the same as mine. She had self-diagnosed OCD and a good sense of direction, just like I did. And she was... my best friend's girl. In another lifetime, maybe even another galaxy, had things not gone so far downhill with Kareem, we probably could've been something special together. I was so deep in thought that I didn't hear the bathroom door open. It wasn't until the frosted glass door to the shower opened that I realized Bianca wanted to join me.

"Good morning, Mr. Baptiste," she said, voice honeyed with lust.

My dick pulsed again, and she looked down and smiled.

"Look, Bianca, we're having a good time together, but you *know* this isn't a permanent situation between us, and you can't stay the night. I have boundaries, aight?"

Bianca nodded. She was a beautiful brown-haired girl with

airbrushed bronze skin and a petite frame. She had big, wide-set, cognac brown eyes, plump lips, a set of perky breasts, and a tight, round ass. She started peppering kisses all over my copper-brown skin, from my neck to my protruding set of eight abs and bellybutton, all the way until she made her way to my dick. She took it and began massaging it slowly while gently flicking her wrists as she approached the head. It throbbed with anticipation in her grasp as she opened her warm, moist mouth and slid me inside.

"Mmm, Psalm, you taste *so* damn good."

"Call me Mister Baptiste," I demanded.

The right side of her lips curled up in a smile before she pushed the loose ringlets of her wet hair from her face and lowered her mouth back down. She swirled her tongue around in slow, sensual circles, teasing me. It was the most intoxicating torture I'd experienced in a while. She tightened her grip around my dick with her jaws and began to move in a swift, up-and-down motion. My breath hitched as my fingertips skated through her soaked mane. She lifted my stiff dick and licked the lining of my nut sack.

My teeth grazed my bottom lip. "Shit, Bianca."

"You like that, Mr. Baptiste?" she asked, following my orders.

I moaned and replied through my gritted teeth. "Yeah, girl."

She shot me a half smile before dropping her hand between her thighs to play with her pussy. The more she played, the harder she sucked, pushing and shoving my wood down her throat while flicking her clit with her middle finger. Her moans bounced off the shower walls as my thighs quaked.

I thrust my thighs toward her face and palmed the back of her head as if her name was Spalding. My morning nut was on the horizon.

"Ahh, shit," I hissed. "Keep sucking. That's it right there."

"Mmm, like this, Mr. Baptiste?" she queried before taking my sack into her mouth and sucking slowly. My balls bounced around in the corners of her warm, wet jaws while I jacked myself off.

I moaned. "Mmm. Come suck this nut out the tip."

She slurped her saliva and spat it back on the tip of my dick just as I leaned forward onto the tips of my toes and delivered a silky mouthful of hot cum to the back of her throat. She swallowed it all in one gulp before sliding my dick out of her mouth and licking me clean. Her warm breath against my sensitive, bare flesh was almost enough to get me started again.

———

After spending most of my Saturday split between the gym and my laptop, I looked at the diamond-studded watch on my left arm to check the time. It was half-past six. I knew I needed to prepare for the rest of the evening's events. Besides, Lotus would *never* let me hear the end of it if I was even sixty seconds late. I closed his laptop and headed to the bathroom to shave and take another shower.

After wrapping my plush towel around my waist, my legs propelled me into my walk-in closet to pick out what I would wear. I settled on my black Armani suit, a black button-up, a black tie, and loafers. I rounded my brush over my coils before smoothing down the sides of my fresh cut. After dousing myself with a few squirts of cologne, my feet went into motion from my condo into the elevator for the parking garage. An unexpected wave of anxiety overcame me when my finger jabbed the button, but I shook it off and proceeded to my car. Close to twenty minutes passed before I arrived at Lotus's restaurant. Instinctively, my eyes darted to my phone for the time. *Good. I've got six minutes to spare.*

I exhaled deeply before checking my reflection in the mirror. My customarily calm brown eyes were steady, and with my poker face covering my sturdy jawline, bushy eyebrows, and mustache that ran around the curves of my lips down to my chin, I was ready for war. I hopped out and handed my keys to the young valet, who didn't look like he could successfully park a tricycle, much less a Mercedes.

"Take care of my baby," I encouraged him.

The jovial valet smiled and nodded. "Yes, sir. I will."

"I'd almost say your car was as good as your taste in women, but we'd both know I'd be lying," a female's voice called out as soon as I sauntered through the automatic revolving glass doors.

I turned to the left to see Lotus standing there looking like the devil herself, red dress and all. Her honey-wheat complexion glowed under the lighting as I studied her heart-shaped face. She had perfectly arched eyebrows that sat in a scowl over her long eyelashes and hazel brown eyes. Her small, turned-up nose and wide-flared, red-painted lips matched the paint on her long, stiletto-pointed fingernails. Her hourglass shape paired well with her petite frame, and her long, dark brown curls flowed carelessly over her narrow shoulders.

"Hi, Lotus," I acknowledged her.

"Were you planning on attending a funeral after our dinner?" she asked, pointing out my all-black attire.

I smirked, instantly brushing off her sarcasm. "We ought to get going."

We stepped into the elevator, and I caught a smile tugging at the corners of Lotus's full lips before she turned away. It wasn't a familiar elevator, but they were all the same in retrospect: lousy lighting, some funky, abstract wallpaper or funhouse mirrors adorning the walls, and the driest elevator tunes. We hadn't been alone for three seconds before my gaze caught hers, and she scoffed. *I can't wait for this fuckin' night to be over,* I thought.

"Is there a problem?" I asked in the most prestigious voice I could muster up.

She scoffed again before wagging her head, shaking the teardrop earrings dangling from her earlobes. Before she could answer, the elevator dinged, and we stepped out to the restaurant's rooftop.

"Let's just get this over with," she muttered before brushing past me to step off the elevator first.

I reached out to grab her arm, instantly slowing her stride. "Hold up a second."

"What?"

"Listen, Kareem wants us to get along, right? Let's try to get through the night like two civil, grown-ass adults. You think you can do that?"

She smacked her lips. "Of course, I can do that. *Can you?*"

Lotus led us to our private table, which was set with two plates, four forks, two knives, three spoons, and two wine glasses at each place, sitting in the quietest section of the restaurant that overlooked the city.

"Of course, I can," I assured her while pulling out her chair.

"Well, aren't you a chivalrous gentleman tonight," Lotus noted before folding her body into the plush chair.

I took my seat and traded glances with her from across the table. There was no denying that Lotus Pierce was a beautiful woman. I couldn't help but notice how her slim frame fit perfectly in her strapless scarlet red, knee-length dress or how she made wings on the corners of her eyelids with her onyx black eyeliner to accentuate her hazel eyes. Simply put, she was astounding.

"Good evening. Can I start you two off with something to drink?" the fair-skinned waitress asked when she approached our table.

She wore a crisp black button-up shirt with a white bowtie and gold-plated name tag with *Raven* printed in bold black font, nameless black pants, and her medium-length red hair pulled back into a neat, low bun.

"Yes, I'll have a glass of Hennessy VS on the rocks, and the lady will have a glass of your finest Merlot."

"Are *you* ready to order?" she asked, unable to hide the desire in her eyes for me right in front of her boss.

Lotus pierced her glare into the frail waitress as if her looks could kill. "We need a minute," she snapped before I could even part my lips to respond.

"No problem. I'll get those drinks right over to y'all," she said, scurrying away.

I shot her a half smile. "If I didn't know any better, I'd say you were jealous."

"You don't know shit. As many hos as I've seen you with over the past year, I shouldn't be surprised, huh?" she challenged, tone sugar-coated with sarcasm.

I shook my head and refocused on the menu before saying something slick. "Do you know what you're going to order?"

A huff burst past her tight lips. "We recently added a new Cajun salmon dish to the menu. I'm going to get that and a garden salad, you?"

"The seafood gumbo," I replied.

A few minutes later, Raven returned with our drinks and took our dinner orders. I handed

her back the menus and nodded politely. She walked away, leaving Lotus and me alone again. An awkward silence hung over us like gray skies on a rainy day as we listened to the live New Orleans jazz band nestled in the corner of the rooftop.

I surveyed the place. "It's been a minute since I've been in here, but it looks good. I like what you've done with the place," I commented.

"Nice to see your investment put to good use, huh?"

"I wasn't going to say that."

"Mmhmm, I bet. So, when are we going to quit tiptoeing around each other and talk about why we're here?" she inquired before taking a sip of wine and leaving a red lipstick stain against the glass.

"So, talk," I insisted, expression stern.

She sighed heavily. "We had an agreement, Psalm."

"This is *not* the time or place to have that conversation, and you know it," I stated uncompromisingly.

"Oh, I think it's the *perfect* place to voice my complaints."

My brow creased. "Complaints? You certainly had no issues with our agreement when my money hit your overdrawn bank account and pulled all the strings to get you in this place, did you?"

She scoffed. "You're such a selfish asshole."

"I always have been."

Her words didn't move me. I valued control and was always prepared to do whatever it took to get the outcome I desired. I felt no sympathy or guilt for most of my decisions, but allowing Lotus to get entangled in the web of deceit I'd spun with Kareem's parents was something I'd never be able to live down.

"Let's be clear, Psalm. It was *you* who came to me, not the other way around. Remember that," she retorted with a hiss and snap of her neck.

"No. *You* be clear, Lotus. You were an escort who was probably one poor decision away from a jail cell or a homeless shelter. I saved you and made your ass an overnight millionaire *and* a business owner. You're *nobody's* victim. Hell, if anything, your ass has got it made in the shade."

"You wouldn't have the balls to fix your lips to say that if you knew the truth."

"What is it, Lotus? What is so bad about your perfect little successful life?" I retorted, ready to shoot down her excuse of bougie misfortunes.

"He beats me," she confessed while lowering her head and her voice simultaneously.

A low growl hummed in my throat. Lotus may have been Kareem's girl, but she was *mine* to damage just as much as she was mine to repair.

THREE

B
e Careful with Me
Lotus

Psalm paused. I could only assume he was trying to digest the words he'd heard fall off my lips. Instead of responding quickly, he cleared his throat while adjusting his tie.

"It's funny, y'know, cards and such. You build, and you build, and you build, and then... *poof*. One soft, delicate gush of wind can tear it down in the blink of an eye. And now, all you've worked for is... nothing. The trick is to choose cheap cards because they have a grainier feel. They're rougher around the edges. Quality ones are smoother and shinier, too, so they slip too easily," he explained before locking eyes with me.

"What does any of that have to do with what I just said?" I interrupted.

"Because I made *you*, Lotus. You're my house of cards, and I'll be damned if I let you knock it down," he said roughly.

As biblical as his name was, Psalm Baptiste was nobody's saint. He was the type of man whose love made me question my sanity.

"Psalm, did you even bother to process what I said?"

"I d–"

I waved my hand to stop him before he could finish his sentence. "Do you know what it feels like to be woken up in the middle of the night gasping for air because his hands are wrapped around your throat, or hearing him calling out names of people you've never met, or being punched in the kidneys and stomach because he thinks you're a fuckin' spy for the enemy?"

"How do I know you're telling the truth?" he quizzed.

"When have I ever lied to you? I-I'm not lying about this, Psalm."

"Then why is this the first time you've bothered speaking about it? Am I supposed to not mention how convenient it is that you accuse him of this right after the final payment from our agreement was wired into your account? If it's more money you want, then just say that."

"There isn't enough money to make me stay one more week with him. What you need to do is run back and tell his parents that their son is a nut job! He's out of everything, no more Prozac, Atrivan, Abilify, nothing. He doesn't sleep, and h-he barely eats. He's a walking zombie, Psalm, and I *didn't* sign up for that."

"That's enough," he muttered, still clearly in denial.

The harder he pushed, the more I was going to pull. It was time Psalm and everyone else knew the truth.

"All he does is work and drink. A year ago, when we signed that agreement, you told me he was struggling with his depression. You said nothin' about the night sweats and the talking in his sleep until four and five o'clock in the morning. I—"

"Goddammit, I said that's enough!" he yelled, slamming his fist down on the table and rattling the sweating water goblets in front of us.

"What's wrong, Psalm? Did the truth make you too uncomfortable? Got you sweatin' in your designer loafers?" I quizzed.

Almost on cue, the waitress returned with our food. We suspended our conversation, forcing polite smiles as she placed our meals on the table.

"Please enjoy your meal and let me know if you all need anything," she said with a smile.

"So, what if he is doing this to you," he considered, finally toying with the thought in his mind. "What do you want me to do?"

"You got me into this; now you need to get me out," I demanded.

"It's not that simple, and you know it."

"Why not?"

"We had an agreement."

"And now it's done. I got my restaurant, and your friend got a year of my life that I'll never get back. I'm sorry, but I'm done."

"You can't be."

"Why not?"

"Because I can't lose him, and I can't lose you either. I need you, Lotus. I need you to stop trying to escape him."

"I want to leave, Psalm," I declared. I was tired of being trapped in a prison of dark, twisted secrets and lies.

Psalm's chocolate brown eyes sliced through me before he announced, "He's going to propose."

My breath hitched as my eyes bulged. If the bomb I'd dropped was big, his was fucking Hiroshima. "*W-what*?" I asked, mouth hanging open.

"Kareem is a... complicated man, Lotus, we all know that. But the truth is, he needed someone, and you agreed to be that someone."

"Yeah, but—"

"And," he continued without batting one of his devilishly long eyelashes. "Collectively, his parents and I made you somebody worth knowing in this city. We made your dreams come true."

Pissed off beyond belief, I shot up from my seat and tossed my napkin down. Psalm bolted upright and rose to meet me, rooting me to the ground. Psalm lifted my chin with his forefinger while burying his gaze deep into my eyes. "It's your choice, Lotus. Are we all gonna win, or are we all gonna lose?"

His words sent a dagger straight to my heart. "I thought you said you loved me. How could you do this?" I muttered as tears glistened in my eyes.

"Sit down and finish your dinner, Lotus."

Psalm reclaimed his seat, leaving me standing by the table for a few meaningless seconds before I lowered myself back down. With my salad fork in hand, my eyes wandered to my plate as I pushed my lettuce around.

Psalm placed his glass back on the table before grabbing my hand. "C'mon, Lo. We've been through this a million and one times."

"You could stop this entire thing by telling him the truth about us. We've been doing this secret dance with each other for far too long."

"That's not part of the agreement that we both agreed to stick to, Lotus," he reminded me.

I pinched my lips together while clenching my jaw. Just because the contract I'd signed had given Psalm the permission to break my heart, it didn't make the damage any less catastrophic. My thoughts swayed between telling him the whole truth and nothing but or keeping it all to myself.

"I was pregnant, Psalm," I announced. "With *your* baby."

He shook his head, refusing to acknowledge truth or reality. He'd been inside me raw probably hundreds of times. I'd rode him backward and forward from sunup to sundown.

When he didn't respond, I continued, "Yeah. That's right. Mr. Big Shot CFO knocked up his *best friend's* girl," I hissed while bending my fingers into air quotes. "I was nine weeks. He killed your child... our child."

His expression went blank. "Why can't you just enjoy your dinner, Lotus?" He scoffed. "All you had to do was show up here, sit, mingle, eat, and then go on with your life. Is that too much to ask?"

I drew a quick breath, feeling myself slowly crumbling under his glare. It was clear he didn't give a fuck about me, at least not in public. I took another sip of wine before crunching a bite of salad between my teeth, trying to keep my composure.

"I can't do this," I announced before pushing my chair away from the table.

He halted me. "Wait."

I paused as a single tear slipped down my cheek. "I don't know why I let you treat me this way."

I watched Psalm take another sip from his drink and a bite of his gumbo before pulling his napkin away from his lap and dabbing his soft lips. "Meet me in the restroom in five."

He got up and walked toward the restroom, leaving me at the table alone. I sat there tapping my red nails on the cream-colored tablecloth while occasionally checking my phone for the time. It was half-past nine. As the minutes passed, the voice in my head kept nagging me. *Why do you let him do you like this? You've always been his little secret, and his lackluster reaction to your confession was proof of that! He doesn't care about you! It's time to wake up and move on!*

Frustrated, I bolted out of my seat toward the elevator. Raven, our waitress, stopped me on my way toward the door.

"Is everything alright, Ms. Pierce?"

I nodded quickly. "Yes, everything's fine. I, uh," I stammered while looking past her. My eyes caught Psalm staring at me from outside the restroom door, and my knees turned to mush. "It's fine."

She shot me a warm smile. "Okay."

I smiled back before making the dick-dizzy decision to change my mind and join Psalm. I pushed open the frosted pane door with the word *Femmes* on the front and stepped inside the large vacant ladies' room while looking around. Across from the door was a black accent wall with red gardenias painted on them. Around the dimly lit corner were three black marble sinks and a large vanity mirror with a few LED pendant lights overhead.

"Show me." Psalm finally broke the silence.

"Show you what?"

"Show me your bruises," he confirmed before locking the door.

I narrowed my eyes at him while folding my arms tightly across my chest. "You think I'd lie about something like that?" I snapped, vexed.

"What I think doesn't matter. You signed a non-disclosure agreement stating that you wouldn't go running to the hills airing the dirty laundry of your troubled boyfriend or his wealthy parents and best friend. Now, show me."

I sucked my teeth, ready to prove him wrong. "Fine! Unzip my dress."

Psalm stepped up and unzipped the tight fabric. As the dress started to open, he sighed and paused. I knew he'd begun to see the dark bruises and marks hidden underneath. "You know he didn't mean it. It's his mind... he's not right."

I blinked to keep the tears in place without looking at him. "I know."

Psalm gently ran the back of his fingers down my spine before taking a few steps back. "Lotus, I *do* love you; I always have, but a deal is a deal. There's just too much on the line."

"I fuckin' hate you, Psalm!"

He slowly wagged his head before stepping close enough to feel my broken heart beating and engulfing me in a warm hug. I collapsed into his care and sobbed harder, allowing the pain to leave my body. In his arms was my favorite place to be.

"Then let me fuck you until you love me again," he whispered against my nape, ensuring I understood that nothing between us had changed.

I looked up at him with tears impairing my vision. That was the problem with Psalm and me; neither of us could let a closed door stay closed for too long. If he couldn't do anything else for me, he could kiss the pain away. My lips were drawn to his like magnets as I kissed him deeply. I didn't resist melting my body into his as Psalm slid my dress over my shoulders and let it fall to my ankles. My fingertips fumbled with his crisp, tucked-in shirt and leather designer belt.

"Which way do you want me?" I asked.

Psalm eyed me hungrily before picking me up by my small waist and placing me on the cold marble counter. His lips came for mine, kissing me roughly as he pulled my lace panties to the side and slid two fingers inside my warmth. He feasted on the sweet spot on my neck while unhooking my bra with one hand and peppering kisses down my chest. Psalm flicked his thick tongue across my honey-brown nipples before sucking on them slowly, as if he had all the time in the world and nowhere else to be. The heat rose between my thighs as he continued to finger fuck me.

A loud moan slipped past my lips as I palmed the back of his head filled with enough dark waves to make anyone seasick.

"I love you so much, Psalm."

"You don't understand how hard this is for me," he confessed as he cupped my breasts in his large hands before gently giving them a slight squeeze.

"Why can't we just be together?" I begged, wanting him to be my knight in shining armor and rescue me.

He lowered his face between my legs, first, gripping my flexed calves before his fingertips skated up my smooth legs and stopped at my throbbing pussy.

"I want an answer, Psalm."

"And I want you," he replied.

Psalm's magic tongue lapped against my clit, causing me to squeal and squirm as if I had ants in my pants.

"You like that?"

"Mmm, yes," I purred.

"Tell me how much."

I gasped for air as I tightened my silky brown thighs around his neck like a boa constrictor, paralyzing him in position. My eyes surveyed him while he feasted on me as if he didn't want to share me with anyone, especially not his best friend. He swirled his tongue around my slit. My moans increased as I gyrated my hips to the sound of his deep slurps. He leaned back and inhaled deeply, taking in the sweet aroma between my sticky thighs before spitting on my pussy. I reached down to spread my lips apart before sliding up and down his face as he sucked on my clit.

"Ahh shit!" I yelled, tugging on my nipples.

He hummed against my pussy, sending chills surging through my body as he ran his full lips over my dripping flesh.

"Ooooh shit, right there, Psalm. Ooooh fuck, I'm about to c-cu-cum!" I squealed as I hooked my right arm under the back of my knee so he could watch me squirt.

He smirked as he made his way back to a standing position, eyes soaking in my naked, quaking body. "Lotus, your body is so goddamn exquisite," he complimented while watching my chest heave in and out. "Now, come get this dick."

I smiled invitingly as Psalm picked me up by my ass cheeks and slid me onto his large, erect dick. My pussy gripped his dick, fitting him like hand in glove.

I moaned while encircling his neck with my arms. "Mmm, baby. You feel so good. I missed you inside me."

He grunted. "Don't you worry, baby. Daddy is gon' fuck all your pain away, I promise."

Psalm's immaculate strength and stamina allowed him to slide his hands underneath my thighs to lift me up and down on his dick with ease. It was as if I was as weightless as a feather in his arms.

"Mmm, yes, Daddy!" I replied, grabbing the sides of his face and pulling his lips onto mine.

I kissed him deeply before biting and sucking on his thick bottom lip. Psalm locked his arms underneath my thighs so that I could bounce freely on his dick. Suspended in midair, I bounced on his dick as my hair slapped against my spine.

I moaned. "Ahh, shit, you feel soooo good, baby. I love you so much."

He placed my left leg on the counter and bent his knees to slide back inside her warmth. Psalm's strong hands engulfed my waist as he stroked me slowly and deeply while staring at my reflection in the mirror. He grabbed a handful of my ass with one hand and a handful of my freely flowing hair with the other, forcing my eyes to meet his.

"Oh shit, baby!" I squealed, nearing my second climax.

Psalm couldn't break his devious stare away from me. His manly hands spread my ass cheeks apart, splitting me open. He stroked me deep before pumping into me harder. I popped my jiggling ass against his dick while grinding back against him and clenching his dick with my walls.

"Fuck, Lotus." He growled.

I knew he *loved* it when I did that shit. Not long after muttering those words, his cell phone started ringing. We both knew it *had* to be Kareem. Refusing to let the moment end, I pushed back harder against him, putting his dick in a chokehold while *praying* he wouldn't answer the call.

"Mmm, shit, girl. I'm about to nut."

"Don't pull out, Psalm. Baby, please, don't pull out," I begged.

"Oooh shit." He groaned as he pushed inside me one last time before violently pulling out and shooting his warm cum all over my lower back. "Keep your legs together while I clean you up." He panted. "He'll be here soon."

Despite the automated burst of lavender and chamomile that sprayed from the corner of the restroom every forty-five seconds, the space was still filled with the pungent aroma of sex, frustration, and lust.

Psalm ran some warm water and took a cloth rag from the opposite side of the counter before cleaning himself off. Then he wiped his semen off my limp body.

"You've got five minutes to get yourself together. Kareem will be expecting you," he stated, pulling up his pants and adjusting his tie. "Kareem will be expecting you."

"And in order for me to say yes and masquerade as a happy, doting fiancée, I want *five million*," I declared, flipping the script.

"That wasn't in the original deal."

"And neither was my hand in marriage. The stakes have changed, and so has my price."

"I'll have to talk to his parents."

"I'm sure they'll say yes if they want to keep him as happy as you claim you do."

"Fine. Whatever it takes to get you down the aisle, consider it done." Psalm shot me a quick nod before unlocking the door and exiting. I pulled up my tight designer dress and discarded my cum-stained panties in the wastebasket. I stepped to the mirror and smoothed my hand against my semi-frizzed hair before reapplying my cherry noir lipstick. My eyes held tears at bay as I dabbed some setting powder on my nose. Last, I sprayed a zig-zag mist of my expensive perfume before stepping through it and back again before leaving the restroom. It was far from our first rodeo in a public setting. Psalm had fucked me in so many bathrooms, coat closets, and elevators I'd lost count. It was about as normal as having sex in a bedroom for us.

My long legs ate up the ground as I returned to the table. I crashed to a halt when I noticed Kareem sitting across from Psalm.

"There she is," Kareem said, eyeing me with a crooked smile.

Kareem stood to greet me, wearing a red Prada button-up with a black and red striped tie, black slacks, and dress shoes. His faint mustache and goatee were trimmed to perfection, and the intense aroma of his expensive cologne screamed *money*. He smoothed his hand over his fresh haircut before kissing my cheek.

"Sit down, baby," he suggested.

"Kareem, what are you doing here?" I quizzed as if I didn't already know.

"I think he was spying on us to make sure we were playing nicely in the sandbox," Psalm answered with a chuckle. "Do you want me to order you a drink, bruh? Somethin' to eat?"

Kareem glanced at the table. "Nah, I'm good, man. Besides, it doesn't look like either of you ate too much of your food as is," he commented.

"I'm about to go to the bar. I'll give you two some alone time," Psalm responded before rising from the table to dodge the heat.

"Alone time? For what?" I asked, not wanting to be alone with Kareem.

"Y'know, time to do things couples do. You already know I don't know nothin' about that," he acknowledged, subliminally reminding me that relationships *weren't* his thing.

Kareem interjected. "Would you like to dance, baby?"

I shot my eyes over at Psalm to see that he'd already turned to walk toward the bar. In a room full of people, I didn't know how I could feel so alone. My chest deflated with a sigh before I responded, "Of course, baby."

We made our way to the dance floor, where the live jazz band played a melodic rendition of "You'd Be So Nice to Come Home To" by Chet Baker. Kareem took me in his arms and crashed his body against mine. He scraped his nose against my neck, drawing in the light aroma of my perfume.

"You smell so damn good, baby," he whispered.

I rested my head on his chest, feeling the imprint of the dog tags he never took off underneath his shirt. "Thank you."

As the band continued to play, I felt Kareem's heartbeat increase as he looked down at me.

"Lo, I know you agreed to meet with Psalm tonight so that you two could bury the hatchet, but I never told you why," he stated.

"I'm listening."

"I wanted you two to get along because I can't have my best friend and *wife* hating each other," he confessed.

"Wife?" I queried, eyes pinning to his.

Kareem stepped back and dropped to one knee while keeping his eyes trained on me. *"If* you'll have me," he asked while reaching inside his pocket and pulling out a black velvet box with a red trim.

I gasped, drawing my hand to my lips. "Kareem, I—"

"Lo, you are my queen, my angel, and the missing piece to my complicated puzzle. And if you marry me, I promise to give you the world."

Even though Psalm had forewarned me about Kareem's proposal, I still felt a sense of nervous energy coursing through my body. I looked down at him. His eyes were calm. His posture was upright, and the sincere expression on his face let me know he was telling the truth. He was ready. He'd seemingly become a changed man overnight, which was more than what I could say for his friend. I tore my eyes over to the bar, where my gaze instantly met Psalm's. He anchored his gaze to mine while taking a sip of his cognac and dipping his chin in a nod.

I forced a smile as my heart broke into a million pieces. "Of course, I will," I answered Kareem.

Kareem stood to his feet and pressed his lips against mine as everyone around us erupted with applause and cheers. "This time is going to be different, baby. I promise I'm going to do everything right. I will be a better man, husband, and everything for *you*. I love you so much," he professed as he slid the fourteen-karat gold engagement ring out of the box and slid it on my finger. It fits like a glove.

Tears came to my eyes for a couple of different reasons. I couldn't help but admire how the princess-cut halo diamond sparkled in the light. I extended my left arm, spreading my fingers to admire the diamonds encircling the band. Even more tiny diamonds surrounded the big one in the ring's center. *Dreams do come true in New Orleans.*

I lightly ran my finger over the scar under his right eyebrow. "I—I love you too," I replied hesitantly, followed by a smile.

FOUR

Heartbreak and Headboards
Psalm

I watched the newly engaged from afar while continuing to sip my drink. Lotus kept her eyes trained on the ring as my best friend whispered sweet nothings in her ear. She and I knew she was more in love with the ring than the man who'd given it to her. Since I met her, I knew I had my hands full with Lotus. Her inability to conform was her one flaw. She'd never been okay playing the game. After all this time, she hadn't learned that the key to making her life easier was to tell people what they wanted to hear. She'd proven time and time again that whatever feelings she felt for me could be suppressed with diamonds and money. The day she couldn't be pacified with material things, we'd all be in some shit. I smirked at the thought before turning my attention back to the female bartender behind the bar.

"Another round, sir?" she asked.

I dipped my chin in a nod. "Hennessy and Coke, please."

I didn't know how I felt about their engagement. On the one hand,

I was happy to see my boy finally smiling again in love, even if we were in love with the same woman. Somehow, I thought pretending to hate her in front of him would make me love her less. I was a fool. I loved Lotus. I'd *always* loved her. I just had a fucked-up way of showing it because I'd made strong alliances to keep Kareem on the straight and narrow, and power and respect trumped matters of the heart every time. Besides, with my companionless ways, I doubted I deserved a serious relationship with any woman, let alone someone I cared about. I'd gone through life mimicking emotions and telling women whatever they wanted to hear. They never had any authority over me. Not like Lotus. She was the only woman I felt true emotions for. Pleasure and pain all wrapped up in one hellishly beautiful woman. I knew I would've looked like a fool if I had tried to talk Kareem out of proposing. My back was against the wall. She didn't have much to choose from between us: a southern playboy and a flawed trust fund baby. Neither of us deserved her.

I forced a smile when I noticed them walking toward me hand-in-hand.

"You two sure know how to cause a scene," I commented once they were in earshot. "Congrats, dawg!"

"Thank you, thank you." Kareem cheesed while dapping me up. "Check out the bling."

He grabbed her left hand and displayed the ring for me to see up close and personal. "That's wassup. It's beautiful."

Lotus nodded. "Thank you."

I stood to my feet to give her a congratulatory hug. It would've been easy to tell her to call off the engagement or give the ring back, but I couldn't. I was the bad guy in our scenario, which meant I had to be the one to make the hard decisions. We'd been stuck in a vicious cycle and playing with fire for too long. My father always used to say *your best teacher is your last mistake.* Her engagement just might've been the thing to save us both.

"I'm going to go ahead and get out of here. Congrats again," I announced before dipping out.

I walked out of the restaurant carrying more than a heavy heart. My mind had run out of space to deal with it all. The valet went to retrieve my car as I put my phone to my ear to get Bianca on the line. The phone rang three times before she answered.

"Yes, Boss."

"It's after hours, B. You don't have to be professional anymore," I reminded her.

"Hi, Papi," she purred into the receiver.

"What you doin'?" I growled, ready to get somethin' started to take my mind off what was plaguing my heart.

"Nothing. My girl is trying to get me to go out with her, but I don't know."

"Why don't y'all come through in about an hour?" I suggested.

"Mmm. What are you trying to get into tonight?"

"You, and maybe your homegirl, too."

———

The pungent, familiar stench of Sour Diesel hung in the air, filling the living room as I waited for Bianca and her homegirl to arrive. I wanted someone to help me lick my wounds. And you know what they say: two heads are better than one. I pulled my blunt again, letting my high pluck me from one end of the spectrum to the other until I didn't know which way was up. I'd been smoking weed and throwing back shots of Hennessy with no chaser since I stepped out of the shower. I poured another shot for the night while I waited. Moments later, my phone dinged with a text from Bianca, letting me know they were on their way up.

"Aight, Psalm, it's showtime," I coached before tossing back the shot glass of cognac.

I ran over to unlock the door before replying to her message to let her know while returning to the couch. I heard the murmur of conversation as they entered my spacious penthouse.

"Hey, Bianca."

She smiled when she saw me seated on the couch. "Hi, Papi."

I smirked back. "Hey, B."

"This is my girl, Nina. Nina, this is my boss, Mr. Baptiste, but..."

"But my friends call me Psalm."

"And *only* I call him Papi," she declared.

"Nice to meet you, Nina," I greeted her with my knee-weakening grin.

The corner of her mouth lifted. "Likewise. You have a nice place."

"Thanks."

"It looks like you already got the party started without us," Bianca stated.

"Ain't no party without y'all. Come sit down and hit this," I encouraged them while patting the empty couch cushion beside me.

Two sets of heels clicked across my floor as Bianca and her friend fully sailed into the living room. Bianca sat beside me while Nina sat on the end. I passed the blunt to Bianca, who hit it a couple of times before passing it to her girl.

"It's nice, right?" I asked.

"Mmmhmm, I like this," Nina said, blowing weed smoke in the air.

The three of us sat there, passing the blunt back and forth until it was reduced to nothing.

"You got anything to drink?" Nina inquired.

"Liquor is in the kitchen. Help yourself."

"Bet." She nodded before bolting away.

"Mmm, Papi, I missed you," Bianca purred. "I wasn't sure you were going to call."

"You know when I call you, you're the one I want... but wassup with your girl?" I mumbled.

Her brows snapped together. "What do you mean?"

"She seems a lil'... uptight. She don't like me?"

Bianca giggled. "No. It's not that. She thinks you're handsome. She told me on the way over here."

"Aight then, just checking."

"Don't worry about her, Papi. I got everything you need right here," she promised before pushing her perky chest against mine.

Our warm bodies fused like s'mores around a campfire as I gave her a kiss filled with nothing but lust. I was faded and yearning to touch her and feel the plumpness of her ass pressed against my fingertips. I didn't want to do much talking or wooing. Besides, romance was foreign to me. I *only* knew how to fuck. Nina stood in the kitchen, trying her best not to watch the show we were putting on in front of her. I could tell she was just as curious as she was uncomfortable.

"As fun as this has been, I'm ready to take this party to the bedroom," I announced while climbing to my feet.

"Let's go then, Papi," Bianca agreed, quickly standing beside me.

"What about you? You down?" I asked Nina while surveying her up and down.

A canopy of long false lashes covered her cat-shaped eyes, which were an intense shade of brown. She wore a short dress that stopped just under the cuff of her ass, exposing everything from her lean, freckled shoulders to her long, tawny brown legs, bronzed to perfection. I licked my lips. She was the portrait of beauty.

She licked the cupid's bow that sat at the top of her lips before speaking. "If you're looking for a happy ending, there's nothing for you here."

"Oh, word?"

"Sorry, but I don't ride the same dicks as my girl."

An adventurous grin spread across my face. "Is that right?" I challenged.

"Yeah. It is," she confirmed with a nod.

"What if I told you I could change your mind?"

"Excuse me?"

"You heard me. What if I could change your mind? Would you let me?"

"What all does that entail?"

"Aht-aht. No more details until you answer the question: would you let me?" I questioned, taking a few steps toward her.

Before answering, she took the shot in her hand and tossed the liquor down her throat before slamming the glass back down on the island. "Fuck it. Why not? We're here to party, right? But I will warn you, I'm a tough cookie to crack."

"Bring that body over here to me," I demanded.

Her hips swayed from side to side as she slowly sauntered toward me. The minute she got within reach, I roughly pulled her kissable mouth onto mine. I felt her melt in my arms as my tongue gently pushed past her lips, exploring her tequila-tasting mouth. As hard as she was playing to get, her body was aching to be touched by a real nigga. I slipped her hand in mine and placed it on my hard dick.

"Would you let me?" I probed, dropping my basketball shorts to the ground while undressing her with my eyes.

Unable to hide her curiosity, she dropped her eyes to my dick. Her teeth sunk into her bottom lip. "I think I'm gonna need another shot."

Before I could respond, I felt Bianca's warm arms slip around my waist before she wrapped her well-manicured fingernails around my shaft.

"Shit, it's so big," Bianca purred.

"*Oy vey!* Veins popping out and shit," Nina muttered before throwing back another shot.

I reached out and ran the back of my hand down Nina's silken skin before extending my hand to hers. "Let's go."

"Lead the way," she replied.

"Can't. You got a nigga mystified by your walk. I can't wait to see it from the back," I admitted while licking my lips.

The innocent sparkle in her eyes made heat surge beneath my skin. I was going to murder her pussy just because I knew I could.

"If it looks this good, then imagine how good it'll taste when I drop my panties and sit it on your face," she teased before placing her hand in mine.

Shit was on and poppin' the minute we hit the bedroom. I had both their sexy asses butt-naked and bent over the balcony ten minutes later. Nina unleashed the freak in her, making Bianca work harder than usual to please me. There was nothing wrong with a little healthy competition, especially when I was the prize.

"You want me to play with your balls while she sucks that fat dick, Papi?"

There was sticky whipped cream on thighs and ice in places so wet and warm it melted upon contact. I was like a kid in a candy store, but instead of lollipops, I was sucking on clits and nipples. I was confident it would be a night I'd never forget.

. . .

"Don't tense up. Just relax your body, and whatever you do, don't run from this dick, or I'll tear your sexy ass apart."

You would've thought it was my birthday by the double scoop of sloppy toppy and pussies I had poppin' on my dick, keeping it standing at attention. I was determined to leave my mark by delivering the most spellbinding orgasms their bodies had ever experienced.

"Mmm, shit. She's sensitive, Papi. You made her cum back to back to back to back."

I turned a half-empty bottle of D'Usse up to my lips, determined to lick until they tapped out. Hearing their sultry moans was like music to my ears. I had them both overdosing on vitamin D, but that wasn't good enough. I wanted to take their *souls* for the night before drowning them in my nut. The shit was almost too X-rated to write about without somebody flagging my shit, ya dig? Let's just say I was one lucky ass mothafucka.

"Just do me one favor. Don't keep that pretty pussy too far from me, aight?"

FIVE

F aking It
Lotus
Six months later.

If there was one thing I loved more than money, it was coffee. I drank it so much that every local coffee shop within a five-mile radius knew me on a first-name basis. As I waited in line, a couple swapped spit directly in front of me. They showed no regard for the people around them who had to suffer through their nauseating PDA. I rolled my eyes while shifting my weight from one heel to another.

"Next in line!" the barista yelled, waving in my direction.

"I'll have the usual," I told her when I approached the counter.

I cracked open my Chanel bag to pull out the matching wallet and handed over my card. The barista swiped it for my purchase of seven dollars and seventy-two cents. My attention drifted back over to the young couple who still hadn't stopped groping each other and kissing every five seconds. It made my stomach churn. There I was, about to get married, knowing I'd never be able to have what they did, at least not with Kareem.

I'd always been the type of person who dictated who I dated based on their astrological sign, occupation, and bank account status. Yeah, materialism was one of my flaws. At least I owned it. The only man who'd ever come into my life and could easily check all the boxes was Psalm. He was everything I'd ever wanted served up on a silver platter. Yet, he was entirely out of reach. Kareem's love for me may have been unconditional, but it was no match for the burgundy and purple bruises he left on my body whenever he had one of his spells or the miscarriage I suffered. I quickly pushed those thoughts to the back of my mind when the barista handed me my iced, sugar-free, vanilla latte with soymilk and a light caramel drizzle.

A smile stretched wide across my lips just as my phone rang. I glanced at the screen to see a picture of my cousin Tiffany and me. With the wedding days away, we'd been spending a hell of a lot more time together than usual. Plus, she was my matron of honor. Because really, who else did I have? I'd been so busy with work I hadn't had time to reach out to her on a personal level. If it didn't have to do with the wedding, I didn't discuss it.

"Hey, T. Wassup?" I answered.

"L-Lo. W-where are y-you?" she sobbed into the receiver.

My eyebrows melted together. "What's wrong?"

"I-it's Ellis. H-he... kicked me out! He said he wants a divorce!"

My brows perched low as I pushed through the coffee shop door. "He *what*?"

"I came home and saw all my shit sprawled out all over the fuckin' lawn! He changed the locks! He won't let me in! The divorce papers were taped to the front fucking door!"

I chewed the corner of my mouth. All the words I wanted to say felt bulky on my tongue. "Where are you now?"

"I'm sitting in my car in the bank parking lot. He took me off all the accounts, too."

"Can he do that?"

"He can do anything he wants when he makes all the money!"

"What about your money? Don't you have your own?" I quizzed, knowing that was one of the things she'd taught me years ago.

"Not enough to keep me afloat for more than a couple of months, three at best."

My chest deflated with a sigh. "Come to my restaurant."

"No. I can't be seen in public looking like this. I'm only driving around in the Mercedes, so nobody tows it away! All my shit is in here! I look like a bougie homeless bitch!" she cried.

Empathy flooded my mouth. "Look, I have to do some hiring anyway. One of the positions I'm looking to fill is for a new general manager. I'll hook you up with a job and put some money in your pocket," I offered.

It was the first time I realized her life wasn't as seamless as I thought it was. The least I could do was put her on payroll for holding me down once upon a time.

"Okay, I'll come. I'm gonna go check into a hotel and be there soon."

When Tiffany arrived at my restaurant, she burst through my office door and fell straight into my arms. Her typically flawless makeup was smeared. Black streaks of her mascara left a telltale trail of tears from her puffy eyes down her rich brown cheeks.

"How could Ellis do this to me?" she quaked, trembling in my arms.

I slowly rubbed her back in soothing circles. "I'm *so* sorry, T."

"After all this time I held him down. His ass wasn't perfect, but he was all I had."

Tiffany sniffled before she pulled away. "Don't be like me, Lotus," she warned. "I fucked up by putting all my eggs in the wrong basket with him."

"So, you're saying I shouldn't marry Kareem?" I inquired.

"You're a grown-ass woman. You can do what you want, but learn from my mistakes."

I heeded her not-so-subliminal warning with a nod. "I still don't understand why he's doing this. You two were happy, right?"

"I thought we were."

Tiffany walked over to claim a seat in front of my desk. I propped myself up on the edge of my desk while examining her closely.

She was only half Black, so her melanated skin was the shade of butterscotch. The tips of her long, wavy hair set right at the top of her breasts. We shared similar features like our smooth button noses and soft pouty lips. The women in our family had always been known for our beauty. Tiffany was no different. She looked beautiful even when she was falling apart.

"What did the divorce papers say?"

She wagged her head. "I haven't even read them. I ripped them off the door so our nosy ass neighbors wouldn't have more to gossip about behind my back."

"Again, I'm so sorry."

"I should be the one apologizing to you."

"For what?"

"For dropping all of this on you. I know your wedding is right around the corner."

"That doesn't matter. You're family, T. I got you," I promised her while sticking out my pinky.

She looped her pinky finger around mine before we both leaned in to kiss them, sealing our pinky promise. "I don't know what I'm gonna do, Lo. Usually, I have my next move lined up, but Ellis threw me for a loop with this shit."

"I know it hurts, but you've got to pick yourself up and move on," I instructed her, trying to give her the same courage and advice she'd given me when Psalm first disappeared.

Her chest deflated. "I don't know if I can."

"You can and you will."

Tiffany shrugged before wiping her eyes with the back of her hand. "If you say so. Thanks for lookin' out for me with the job. I won't let you down."

I rested my hand on her shaking shoulder. "You're my cousin, and I love you dearly, so the job is here when you're ready. Take the next few days to get your mind right, and then come in here refreshed and with that hustle mentality you've always had. I already know you're gonna be the best employee I have here."

"I thought I was more to you than just another employee on your payroll."

I clicked my tongue. "You know me well enough to know not to take everything I do and say so literal."

———

After Tiffany left, I got swept up in back-to-back interviews for new servers, responded to endless emails from vendors, and did as much work as possible before my time off for the next few weeks. I worked through lunch and found myself eating stale candy hearts I'd found in the back of one of my desk drawers from last Valentine's Day. *It will have to do. I'm on a diet anyway.* My wedding day was less than seventy-two hours away. Most women dreamed of the day they'd get to put on *the* dress of their dreams and walk down the aisle to the man who still gave them butterflies in the pit of their stomachs. Unfortunately, true happiness was the only luxury I didn't have. It was true what they said: money couldn't buy happiness.

My phone vibrated against the desk, causing me to glance at the screen. It was Kareem. I rolled my eyes skyward for thinking him up before answering in a tone that was neither excited nor annoyed. "Hello?"

"Hey, you busy?"

"Very, but what's up? What's wrong?" I asked.

"Nothing is wrong. I wanted to get out of the office in time to surprise you at the restaurant to take you somewhere for lunch, but I ended up working through it. It's a madhouse over here. I don't know what they will do without me here for the next few weeks once we leave for our honeymoon."

"Yeah, I bet. It's the same here."

Shortly after our engagement, Kareem started as a financial consultant at Psalm's bank. I was grateful the promotion gave him more responsibility, which kept his mood stable.

"Yeah, but I just wanted to call and see how your day was going."

I huffed. "It's okay."

"Everything okay?"

"Everything is fine. I'm just trying to enjoy my last few minutes of peace and quiet before I return to work," I answered.

"I feel that. I'll let you go then."

"Okay, I'll talk to you later."

"Oh, and Lo?"

"Yeah, Kareem?"

"Can you call the planner and have them set one more place setting at the reception?"

I frowned. "For who? The wedding is three days away!"

"I know, I know, but it's for Psalm's date. You know how last minute he is."

I cleared my throat. "His *what*? I thought you said you talked to him, and he said he wasn't bringing anyone."

"I did. He just hit me with this shit like twenty minutes ago. Besides, he's my best man. I can't have him out here lookin' lonely at *my* wedding."

"Who is it? I mean, who is he bringing?"

"His assistant, Bianca."

I pressed my lips into a hard line as I sighed. It didn't take a rocket scientist to figure out Psalm had been sticking his dick inside Bianca since her first day of working for him. Regardless, she was a nonfactor.

"I'll see what I can do, but I'm not making any promises. You know I don't like that last-minute shit," I hissed.

"I know, baby. Thank you. Have a good rest of your day."

"Thanks, you too," I replied as my phone beeped, letting me know I had one percent left on my battery.

"I love you."

"I—I love you too," I replied as my phone went dead.

I sighed while reaching across my desk to plug in my phone. I was up until three in the morning, looking up flights to get as far away from Kareem, Psalm, and everyone else. I wanted to be as far away as possible on the morning of my wedding day. I couldn't stop thinking of packing a bag and jetting off on our honeymoon solo. I was ready to be on my runaway bride shit. The only thing stopping me was having to deal with the wrath of Psalm *and* Kareem's parents when they realized I'd left their son spiraling at the altar.

The knock on my door jarred my thoughts back to the present. "Come in."

The door flung open, revealing my assistant, Candice, on the other side. Instead of saying anything, she just held up a small white envelope. I instantly recognized it. I'd been getting random notes delivered to my restaurant for the past few weeks leading up to the wedding. They all said the same chilling thing: *I know the secrets you're keeping from your prince charming. Call off the wedding and run, or I'll air all your dirty laundry.*

"Another one?" I quizzed.

She nodded. "Yup. This is the third one, right?"

"Fourth."

"Have you said anything?"

"No. I have it under control," I lied. "Rip it up and throw it in the trash."

———

The rest of my workday zoomed by. It seemed like all I'd done all day was put out one fire after the next. I was in the stockroom in the back, going over the latest inventory list with Candice, when my stomach began to churn. I wrapped my arms around myself and hunched over.

"You sure you okay, Boss Lady?" Candice asked with a questioning brow.

I set the clipboard down while nodding slowly as my insides tumbled into each other. "Mmhm. Actually, excuse me."

I shot up on unsteady legs, ran toward the restroom, and wretched into the nearest toilet. Once I was sure I was done, I headed to the sink to wash my hands and rinse out my mouth. I'd been feeling a bit off for a little over a week. My stomach was queasy as butterflies tormented my gut night and day. Even the slightest smells would make my stomach roll. After drying my hands, I shook off the excess water and went back into the stockroom.

"Sorry about that," I told Candice.

"All good now?"

I dipped my chin. "Yup. I'm all good now," I assured her.

Although we were alone, Candice stepped closer to me and kept her voice low. "Forgive me for overstepping, but could you be pregnant?" she quizzed.

I snapped my eyes at her before softening my gaze. She was only trying to be helpful. Besides, her question sent a thrill of possibility zinging through me. "Run to the store and get me a test. And be discrete about it, okay, Candice?"

She dipped her chin. "On it."

Twenty minutes later, Candice returned with a box of two tests. She discretely passed the bag to me, and I went into the bathroom to take it before locking myself inside my office. The three-minute timer on my phone dinged, and I eagerly shot over to my desk to see the results. A wide grin exposed my teeth as I picked up the test. According to the instructions on the box, I *was* pregnant.

I stepped outside my office to see Candice standing there. "Well?" she asked.

I looked around before quickly pulling her back inside. "Read it and make sure I'm not trippin'."

"Where is it?"

"Over there," I answered, pointing to the edge of my desk.

Candice walked over and picked up the instructions with one hand and the test with the other. After looking over both, she turned back to me.

"Well?" I urged.

"You're definitely pregnant. See the two lines right there, bold and beautiful?"

I bobbed my head. "Oh. Okay then."

"Are we happy about this or..."

"I don't know yet."

"Okay then," she answered, taking that as her cue to leave. "I'll give you a minute to process all this."

"Thanks, Candice."

"No problem."

Was I happy to be carrying Psalm's baby? Absolutely. Was I thrilled about the timing of it all? Absolutely not. But what could I do? After pulling away from the curb outside the front of my restaurant, I drove to the hotel where Tiff was staying. I promised I'd check in on her, and I wanted to make good on my word. I decided against telling her about my pregnancy. With all she was going through, I didn't feel right adding my drama to her already heavy load. On the drive, I toyed with the idea of calling Psalm and telling him I was pregnant again. By the time I arrived at Tiffany's hotel, I *still* hadn't made the call. It was something he needed to hear in person. So, I decided to tell him the next time I saw him. Instead, I called my cousin. The phone rang four times before Tiff answered.

"Hello?" she answered groggily. I couldn't tell whether she'd still been crying or she was asleep.

"Hey, I'm outside. You want me to come up, or were you asleep?"

She cleared her throat. "I'm awake. You can come up if you want."

"You know what, why don't you come back to my place?" I suggested.

"For what?"

"I don't think you should be alone, at least not for the night."

She huffed. "I'm fine. Well, I'm *not* fine, but I will be."

"Can you please come? If only for the night? I'll drive you back in the morning if you want."

"Why do you keep pushing this?"

"Because I'll sleep better knowing you're okay."

She let out a long breath into the receiver. "I only had enough money for one night anyway. With the day I've had, I just needed one last night in the comfort of a five-star living situation. Taking a nap in my car in the parking lot earlier left a crick in my damn neck," she complained.

"Even more reason to come home with me! Come on!"

"Fine. I just got out of the shower not too long ago. Let me throw something on and gather my shit. I'll be down in ten to follow you to your place."

"All right. I'll be waiting."

Tiff and I sailed through the front door, giggling when Kareem's voice sounded off in the darkness before I could flip on the light.

"Where you been, Lo?" he challenged.

I jumped as my eyes shot up toward him. "Kareem!" I yelled, fingers sprawled across my chest as my heart thumped. "You scared me!"

He folded his muscular arms across his chest, doubling down on his initial statement. "I'm waiting for my answer."

I stepped aside so that he could see Tiffany, hoping he'd stop embarrassing my ass. "Kareem, this is my cousin, Tiffany. She's the matron of honor at our wedding. I've invited her to stay the night with us."

"Hey, there, my soon-to-be cousin. You have a beautiful home," she complimented while glancing around.

"Thank you," Kareem mumbled.

I turned to face Tiff. "I'm sorry. Can you give us a minute? The guest room is upstairs, first room on the right," I explained.

"Sure."

Once my cousin was out of earshot, Kareem started up again. "I called the restaurant. Candice said you left an hour ago."

"Okay, and?"

He advanced toward me, narrowing the space between us. I instinctively backed up. "*And* where were you? Where'd you go after you left the restaurant? We only live twenty minutes from there."

I frowned while folding my arms over my stomach for protection. "Are you being serious right now? Did you not see me walk in here with my cousin? I was with her!"

He unclenched his jaw. "All I'm saying is, as your husband, I deserve to know where you are at all times!"

"I'm not your wife, *yet*!" I reminded him with a hiss, a curse hot on my tongue.

He snapped his brows together and narrowed his whiskey-colored eyes. "What the fuck does that mean? Huh? You wanna call off the wedding? *Why*? Because you cheatin' with some other nigga? Huh? Is that what you were out there doing? Ho-ing around?" he accused.

I huffed. As badly as I wanted to bark back on his ass, I had too much on my plate and too much on my mind. My main priority was protecting the new life growing inside me. The baby was going to be my one-way ticket away from Kareem and back into the arms of his best friend.

"Listen, baby. I'm just tired, okay? This wedding has me stressed the fuck out, so after I left the restaurant, I went for a silent drive to clear my head, since you *must* know."

He eyed me suspiciously for a few seconds before relaxing his tensed shoulders. "Are you sure that's all?"

"Of course, I am. I'm just trying to get through the next few days without pulling out my hair and each one of my eyelashes, especially when you got me doin' last-minute shit for the wedding on behalf of *your* best man," I reminded him.

Kareem huffed before walking over and pulling me into his arms. "I'm sorry, baby."

"Are you? Because a minute ago, I was the biggest ho in NOLA," I retorted before pushing him away.

"I'm sorry, Lo. I mean it. I guess I'm stressed about this wedding too."

"Yeah, well, your ass got a funny way of showin' it."

"Let me make it up to you. What would make it better, baby? You name it, and it's yours."

I paused. "*Well,* there is this new Chanel bag I've had my eye on for a while... and the fact that my cousin's husband kicked her out and she has nowhere to go, so I'm hoping you'll agree to let her stay here for a few months until she can get back on her feet?" I asked, speaking so quickly I was rambling.

"Would that make you happy?"

I nodded. "She looked out for me at a hard time in my life, and I wanna pay it back."

"Then okay, your cousin can stay."

"Thank you." I smiled at him before prancing back to the guest room and knocking on the door. "Good news," I told Tiffany once we were face to face.

"What?"

"It's official. You can stay with us for a few months or however long it takes you to get on your feet."

She sighed before a ghost of a smile crept up on her face. It was the first time I'd seen her smile all day. "Thank you, Lo. Thank you so much, and please, thank Kareem for me too. I know how stressful of a time things are for y'all right now. And taking on an unexpected house guest a few days before your wedding? You're both saints in my eyes."

I snickered. "I'll tell him. Listen, I'ma go take a shower. I'll check on you before I go to bed."

"Okay."

"Mmkay."

"Hey, Lo?"

"Yeah?" I asked, turning back to face her.

"I lied to you before," she admitted.

"What are you talking about?"

"I know why Ellis wants a divorce."

I stepped back inside the guest room and closed the door behind me. The painted wood was cold against my back as I rested against it. "Why?"

"I was having an affair… and this isn't the first time."

My eyes doubled in size. "W-what? With who? Why?"

"He forgave me the first time, but he always said if he *ever* caught me again, he'd take everything from me. So, when he caught me with my hand in the cookie jar this time, well, let's just say I know first-hand what they mean when they say don't bite the hand that feeds you."

"Shit, T. What about the guy you were sleeping with? What happens with him now?"

She huffed. "I know what I'm about to say is going to sound terrible, but it was only fun because it was a secret. Now that the *one* person who wasn't supposed to find out about it did, I don't think it hits the same, at least not for me."

"So, then, why not work on your marriage with Ellis? You said he took you back once, right? Maybe he could find it in his heart to do it again."

"Oh, Lo. You've always had such a heart of gold. But the real world don't work like that. He already gave me my second chance. He's made it clear I won't get a third."

"No disrespect, but can I ask why you did it?" I inquired.

"Did what? Cheat?"

I nodded to confirm. "Yeah. I mean, you say you love him."

"What's the one thing I always used to tell you?"

"You used to tell me a lot of things."

"Not like this."

I paused for a few seconds, allowing my mind the time to think back. "Never fall—"

"Never fall in love for free," she answered, talking over me.

"What's that got to do with my question?"

"When things were good with Ellis, they were great. He was at the top of his game in real estate. He was literally making money in his sleep. But when the market dried up, so did his pockets. It's been a hard few years, and like I said, this isn't our first rough patch."

"When was the first?"

She huffed. "A *long* time ago. That's all that matters. You would've thought I learned my lesson, but here I am, back at square one, like I'm not pushing thirty."

"At least tell me the nigga you was fuckin' on recently was paid," I said, hoping for a silver lining.

"Oh, trust, he is."

"Then it sounds like you need to turn your plan B into your plan A."

"Yeah. You might be right about that. I don't know. You know I'm always scheming. I'll land on my feet."

"You always do."

She shot her eyes up to me. "Yeah, so do you."

I smiled. "Must be in our blood."

"Must be, cousin."

"Try to get some sleep, okay? We'll talk more in the morning."

"Yeah, thanks. You too."

SIX

Two Wrongs Don't Make a Right, but I Don't Give
a Damn
      Psalm

I strolled into the restaurant fifteen minutes late for Lotus and Kareem's rehearsal dinner. To my surprise, it hadn't started yet.

"Psalm, you're here!" Kareem's mom called out to me.

I reached out to hug her with a fake smile plastered across my face. "Hey, Mama," I greeted her with a kiss on the cheek.

After my parents died in a car accident when I was eighteen, Kareem's parents stepped up to fill their shoes. I spent every Christmas, every Easter, and a week every summer visiting them after I went to college. The Solomons were my home away from home.

"We're almost down that aisle!" she cheered, all smiles.

My chin dipped. "I know!"

In another twenty-four hours, Lotus would be Mrs. Kareem Solomon, five million dollars richer, and we'd *all* be off the hook.

"Thank you so much for all this. God knows where we'd be without you, Psalm. I mean that. You've been a godsend to our family."

A trace of a smile brushed my lips. "Thank you, Mama. That means a lot."

"Now, where are the bride and groom? Every time I get my eyes on one, I lose the other!"

"I don't know. I'll try to find them."

"When you do, let them know we're in the private section in the back. We're still waiting on her matron of honor, Tiffany, to show up," she informed me.

The name came past my ears and went as I found another smile for her. "Cool. I'ma go see about Kareem."

"Thanks, baby."

I shoved around on the ball of my foot while surveying the large, upscale restaurant. My legs slowly approached the front when my eyes landed on Lotus. She looked as beautiful as always. As much as I wish I could say I kept my distance from her since her engagement, I couldn't. That was too much like right. I broke her back the night of their engagement party. I sexed her crazy in the hotel room next door on her girls-only bachelorette getaway. I sweated out her curls on the balcony after her bridal shower brunch. I couldn't get enough. It was almost as if the ring on her finger made me want her more because I knew our time together was coming to a close.

Her legs propelled her over to me with a serious expression across her face. "Psalm, I'm glad you're here. Can we step outside?"

"Have you seen Kareem?" I quizzed.

Her brows snapped together. "I think he's at the bar. Can we step outside? There's something I need to talk to you about."

"Can it wait? Mama wants me to put eyes on Kareem."

Her weightless curls shook as she wagged her head. "No. It can't."

I agreed, seeing as we were only a few feet from the exit. "Fine. Let's go." Once we got through the door, we stepped off to the side. "What is it?"

"We have to call off the wedding," she announced.

"What?" I asked, smacking my lips. Lotus's childish antics were the last thing I needed or wanted to deal with.

"Is this about the fuckin' money?"

"No."

"Then what the fuck, Lotus?"

"You'd know if you listened to me!"

I wagged my head with my brows snapped together in disapproval. "I don't want to! Your wedding is tomorrow! I've already arranged for the money to be sent to your account once you say I do. You can't back out now, yo! You can't do this!" I argued.

"We have to call the wedding off because I'm pregnant, Psalm. And before you ask, the baby is yours. He hasn't touched me in that way in a long time," she confirmed.

My brows wrinkled. "*What*?"

My hand slipped down my face. I was speechless. I'd been dipping and slipping in that pussy like I'd never dipped and slipped before. I was certain we'd have a hefty price to pay for the dirt we'd done, but a *baby*? I knew better than to question the paternity. It would be hard to deny a kid who looked just like me. I stood with my feet cemented to the pavement, waiting for the camera crew to jump out from behind the bush and tell me it was all for an online skit, and I'd been punk'd. That shit never happened.

Lotus continued, "I found out a couple of days ago."

My forehead wrinkled. "Why would you wait until now to say something? I mean, damn, Lotus! What do you want me to do with this information the night before your wedding?"

"I want this baby to know who its real father is, Psalm, so I'm telling Kareem tonight. I just wanted to give you the courtesy of telling you first since *you're* the father."

I reached out to grab her hands before dropping them. Her news had fucked me up so much I'd forgotten we were in public.

My gaze pinned to hers. "Lotus, *please* don't do this. Please. Think about what you're losing. If you walk away now, there's no more money. The well will run dry. On top of that, you'll have to explain this to his parents."

The glimmer in her eyes extinguished. "I can't walk down that aisle knowing the truth."

"Lotus–"

She waved her hand to silence me. "I can't."

My burning eyes remained trained on her. "So, this is how you want it to go down, huh? You'd do this to me?" I accused.

"*What*? What am I doing to you?"

"We'll lose everything if Kareem finds out we've been messing around behind his back! Telling him the truth may clear your conscience, but it won't do anything but blow up the rest of our lives. Is that what you want?"

Lotus drilled her teary gaze into mine, refusing to let a tear slip. "What do you want me to do?"

"Marry him," I answered.

"And what about the baby?"

I reached out for her hands again. "We'll figure out the baby, Lotus. I promise we will, but you cannot back out on me now. Promise me you'll be at the church tomorrow."

She sniffled before sliding her hands out of mine and pushing past me. "Fuck you, Psalm."

I walked back inside a couple of minutes later, still unsure how I felt about the news of Lotus being pregnant by me for a *second* time. Before I had time to process it, I spotted Kareem sitting at the bar in the middle of the restaurant. He had his tie in one hand and a glass of liquor on ice in the other. His sad eyes landed on mine as soon as I approached him. He shot me a quick nod before slinging back his drink.

"Damn, man. You drinking without me?" I quizzed.

"Tell the bartender to pour up another one then," Kareem replied.

I sat beside him while waving down the bartender for another round. Once we had fresh drinks, I raised my glass and smiled. "Here's to your wedding."

Instead of returning the smile, Kareem simply shook his head. "If there is going to be one."

I gave him a once-over. His haircut was fresh. He was almost entirely dressed. The only thing missing was his undone tie hanging loosely around his collar.

"What's up, bro? Don't tell me you got a case of cold feet."

"It's not me," he answered before throwing the next shot back.

"Huh? What's going on? Why don't you have your tie on?" I probed all in one breath.

"Yo, let's go outside. I gotta holla at you about something."

"What? What's wrong?" I asked, dreading having to go back outside.

"It's Lotus."

"What about her?"

He looked over his shoulder before answering. "I followed her yesterday."

My brows heightened. "*What?*"

"Lotus. I followed her."

"I heard you. Why?"

"She's been acting strange for the past few weeks now. She doesn't want me to touch her. She's sleeping in the other room or on the couch and then claims she was too tired to come to bed. I don't know what to do," he answered with stress all in his expression.

"What happened when you followed her? What'd she do?"

"Nothin'."

"*Nothin'?*" I quizzed.

He wagged his head. "Nope."

I frowned. "Then why the fuck we talkin' about this shit?"

"Because I can't shake this feeling in my gut, nigga."

I sucked my teeth. "It sounds like wedding jitters to me, my boy."

"Nah. This ain't no cold feet shit, Psalm. It's more than that. I'm thinking about hiring a private investigator," he informed me.

"That's a little O.D., don't you think?" I quizzed while running my hand over my beard. Knowing she was carrying my baby, I couldn't have him hiring anyone who would blow up his life and ours.

"Is it?"

"Bruh, you just stood here and told me that you followed the woman you're about to marry *tomorrow* around the city and saw *nothing* to justify whatever is happening in your head. And I'm telling you that you wildin'."

He cocked his head to the side. "You really think I'm trippin'?"

"A hunnid percent," I answered while patting his shoulder. "I'm your boy. Would I lie to you?"

"I don't know, man."

"Lotus loves you, Kareem. She'll be a good wife for you," I assured him, trying to put his suspicions to ease. "Besides, take it from the professional single nigga, ain't nothin' for you out in these streets. Go on and get your queen."

Kareem brushed his hand over his head as his chest deflated with a long sigh. "Yo, thank you, Psalm."

"Aye, say less."

"Nah, I'm for real. You don't know how much I love and appreciate you for sticking with me all these years. You're more than my right hand; you're my brotha."

We stood to our feet and dapped each other up before he pulled me into a quick hug. "Let's get our asses back to your section before Mama come over here fussin' at me for lettin' you miss dinner." I chuckled.

He patted my back with a smile. "You right."

After our conversation, a part of me knew I was on the brink of losing something. I'd done too much dirt to expect anything less. I didn't know if it would be my best friend, the woman I loved, or my happiness. It was only a matter of time before the universe slung some shitty karma my way. And you know what they say about karma. That bitch is a mothafucka.

SEVEN

N.A.S.
Lotus

I *hated* Psalm for his reaction. Just thinking about it set my skin on fire, but then again, I wasn't really that surprised. Looking back, I knew I could've been more tactful in my delivery, but I was running out of time and options. I wanted to raise my baby with the man I loved, and I wanted it to call him Daddy, not Uncle. Most importantly, I wanted to keep my baby safe. The main reason I chose to keep the baby was because I wanted to ensure Psalm chose me in all the ways I'd already chosen him. Our child was the only lifeline left between us.

I stood in the mirror wearing my white silk robe with my hair and makeup freshly done. I refused to blink while staring at the white dress hanging up against the door. The wedding day I'd been dreading since the night Kareem slid the diamond ring on my finger had finally arrived. Between my cousin and Kareem's family invading my space, I hadn't had a moment alone to collect my thoughts. Anxiety swirled around my head like a carousel as I sat on the edge of the couch, silently plotting my escape.

"You okay, girl?" Tiffany asked.

I wagged my head. "You were right. I can't put all my eggs in one basket, T. I can't do this."

"*What?*"

I leaned in closer to her. "I haven't told anybody about this, but I've been getting notes delivered to the restaurant for the past few weeks."

Her brow creased. "Notes? Saying what?"

"They always said the same thing: that someone knows my secrets, and if I married Kareem, they'd air *all* my dirty laundry."

Tiffany stared at me with wide eyes. "What the fuck, Lo? What do you think that even means?"

I wagged my head. "I-I don't know."

I felt the warmth of Tiff's hand on my bare shoulder. "Maybe it's nothing."

"What if it isn't?"

"You know what all this sounds like to me?"

"What?"

"A case of cold feet," she whispered. "You'll be fine."

"No. You don't understand. None of you understand!" I yelled as I sprang to my feet.

Tears poured down my cheeks, instantly ruining my makeup.

The room instantly went silent as everyone stared at me with wide eyes. Feeling the crimson flushing into my cheeks, I lowered my head in embarrassment. I'd kept the news of the notes a secret up until then. But between that, the baby, and my pending five-million-dollar payout, there was so much white noise in my head I couldn't think straight enough to form words. My head felt too heavy for my shoulders to bear.

"I'd trade places with you if I could, but I can't, so just let me know what you want me to do, and I'll do it," she declared. "You wanna stay, or you wanna go?"

I sighed, hearing the disappointment in her voice. I pressed my red lips together tightly before dabbing my eyes with the back of my hand. "I just need a minute... or three."

"Okay. Take as much time as you need. I'll go get you some water or something stronger."

I wagged my head, knowing she didn't know about the baby. "Thanks... water is fine."

Minutes later, I turned back toward the door when I saw Tiffany clutching a glass of ice-cold sparkling water. I was grateful but *wished* it was something more potent. I needed something to put me in a drunken stupor and get me down the aisle. *It's going to be okay. It's all going to work out in the end. All you have to do is say two little words, Lo, just two little words.* No matter how often I kept repeating the same thing, my heart knew otherwise. Contrary to what it looked like, I *was* a one-man girl, at least I wanted to be. There was *no way* I could spend the rest of my life with Kareem when I knew Psalm was the one I was really in love with.

"What's going on up there, Tiff?" I quizzed.

"I won't lie. People are getting antsy since the wedding was supposed to start almost thirty minutes ago. What do you want me to tell them?"

"Tell them I need more time! I'm not coming out until I'm ready! If ever!"

"Okay, okay, just stay calm. I told you to take all the time you need. If he loves you like he says he does, he'll wait. I'll go tell him."

I bobbed my head. "Thanks, girl."

"Now, drink up and relax," she encouraged. "It'll all be over soon."

Tiffany disappeared again, and I set the water down, unable to stop my hands from shaking long enough to take a sip. As badly as I wanted to calm my nerves, I couldn't stop my tears from falling. My hands fiddled in my lap until she returned. A few moments later, I heard an impatient knock on the other side of the door.

"Who is it?" Tiffany called out.

"It's me, Psalm. I came to talk to Lotus. Can I come in?" he asked.

Tiffany made a face before cracking the door open a sliver. "What do you want? I already told Kareem she needs more time," she snapped at him.

"That's fine. I didn't come down here to start any drama. I was just hoping I could talk to her."

My heart backflipped in my chest. *Is he here to rescue me?* "It's fine. Let him in," I announced.

The door opened, and Psalm sauntered in, shifting his tie while clearing his throat. "Can we get a minute alone?" he requested.

"It's fine," I announced.

Psalm patiently waited until everyone cleared out of the suite, then locked the door. He walked back over to me and closed the gap between us. "What the fuck are you doing, Lotus?" he challenged sternly, unamused by the tears that filled my swollen, red eyes.

"Excuse me?"

"You heard me! You've got Kareem upstairs about to blow a gasket because he thinks you don't want to go through with this wedding!"

"I *don't*! I've been telling you this for months! You obviously haven't been listening!" I accused.

He lifted my chin and stared at me with a blank expression written across his face. "You can, and you will."

My mind went blank as I stared back into his eyes. A part of me regretted allowing him to see me in my bag of emotions, but I wore my feelings for him like a second skin. I had to find a way to get him to see we were meant to be together. If not for me, then at least our unborn child.

"What about our baby, Psalm? Don't you want to be a family? Tell me you don't, and I'll walk down that aisle right now and marry Kareem."

Psalm's icy white teeth sunk into his bottom lip as he let his hands fall back to his side. I watched his eyes dart over to the glass of water I still hadn't managed to take a sip of. "Have you been drinking?"

"It's water. Don't change the subject!"

He walked over and picked it up to further examine it before taking a sip. "And so, it is."

I scoffed. "Why do you care what I do anyway?"

"Because you're mine!" he roared. "It doesn't matter if you walk down that aisle and become his today. You'll be mine forever."

"Why can't you just say you love me?"

"It's not that simple, and you know it, Lotus! We've been through this time and time again! You're with Kareem for his health. Do you want him to die, huh? Do you? Do you want him to kill himself because you decided to be selfish and put your needs above his?"

I huffed, knowing what was about to fall off my tongue would be harsh, but they were the truth. "If him dying means I get to live the rest of my life being true to myself by being with the man I love, then yes, Psalm. I want him to die."

Psalm took a few steps back in shock. "I can't lose him, Lotus. Not like this."

"And I can't lose you. At least not until I've had the opportunity to have you fully," I confessed as tears sparkled in my eyes.

"Have you ever had a best friend, Lotus? I mean a *real* best friend. Someone that you would do anything for, no matter what it was. Yeah, I know what the two of us are doing, and the things we're feeling aren't right. They're not! I've tried to keep my distance from you, for your sake and his."

"And what about you, huh? Who's looking out for Psalm? You think Kareem would do this for you if the roles were reversed?"

His broad shoulders rose and fell. "I can only hope he would."

"*Hope*? That's not good enough!"

Psalm chugged the rest of the water into my glass before throwing it across the room. "It's all I can fuckin' give you, Lotus! I'm sorry, but I made a conscious decision to put my feelings to the side for the sake of my friend, and I *can't* go back on my word!"

I flung my engagement ring across the room and watched it roll across the hardwood floor. Psalm may have had a temper, but I had no filter. "Take it! I don't want it! I don't want any of it! Fuck all of this, Psalm! I'm done! I'm tired!"

"Tired of what? Having a man who would give his life for you? A man who loves you more than I ever could?"

All the breath in my lungs vacated my body when I heard those words. "Psalm..."

"No! That's some truth for your ass, Lotus! He's been going to therapy faithfully, taking his meds, and working full time! What more do you want from him?"

"I want him to be you!" I yelled.

"Life ain't about always gettin' what we want. We had what we had, and now that's over. We both need to move on."

"I didn't sign up for this, Psalm!"

"Actually, you did," he rebutted.

I scoffed while shaking my head in disgust. Psalm Baptiste was living proof that niggas really ain't shit.

Chapter Eight—Happily Ever After Will *Always* Fail

Psalm

Lotus cut her teary eyes at me. "You know what, you're right. So, he's not the zombie he was a year ago. But what happens when he runs out of meds or decides he no longer wants to go to therapy, which he says at least once a week, in case you didn't know!"

My jaw tensed. "*You* take him to therapy and the doctor. *You* pick up his prescriptions. *You* chop them up and put them in his food like a fucking child if you have to! Because *you're* about to be his wife in a few minutes! It's your job to care for him because it's what you've been paid to do!" I hissed.

"And who's going to take care of me, Psalm? Huh? Who? Because it damn sure hasn't been you!"

I brushed my hand over my jawline. "What the fuck do you want from me, Lotus?"

She looked into my eyes with a look of defeat across her face, all but begging me to see she'd been wearing her heart on her sleeve for me. As emotionally unstable as she looked, it wasn't hard for me to see the beauty behind her eyes.

"I want you to give a fuck about me and this baby!" she pleaded.

"I didn't say I didn't give a fuck."

The only thing that kept replaying through my head was if I could take it on the chin and watch my firstborn be raised by my boy. Could I just be known as Uncle P or godfather?

"You didn't have to! I'm begging you to save us, Psalm! Please, I *need* you..."

"I've been trying to do things the right way. I thought it would make it easier for the both of us, but…"

"But what?" she asked with hope laced in her voice.

I shifted my weight from one leg to the other while internally swatting away my feelings for her like a flying insect. It didn't matter how much distance was placed between us; I simply couldn't see my life without her in it. Our eyes met at the same time as our palms. With interlocked fingers, I closed the gap between us until our chests met. What Lotus and I shared was taboo, forbidden, and downright disrespectful. Yet, neither of us could stop it from happening. I was ready to compromise who I was and all I stood for for her. I kept my gaze trained on her while standing frozen in place. I knew the minute I moved, I would attack her, and we'd wind up doing something I wasn't sure either of us would regret.

"But… *if* this is our make-or-break moment, I think we owe it to ourselves to seize it. Because the minute we walk out that door, everything will change."

"Psalm… kiss me," she whispered.

I dropped her hands to envelop her waist, tightening my grip as I brought my lips within the same breathing space as hers.

"This is a bad idea," I whispered against her red-painted lips.

"I know."

"Then we should stop."

"We *should*…"

"But I can't," I admitted.

"Me either."

My lips met hers, and I kissed her gently, just like I did the first time we met. It was only right our last kiss held as much weight as our first. Lotus's body instantly melted into mine, giving me every last drop of herself. I recklessly tore my fingers through her head full of beautiful curls as she fumbled with my belt to unhook my pants. There we were again, playing with fire. I couldn't lie. I got off on the thrill.

"I hate that I love you," Lotus whispered as she pulled her lips away from mine.

"I love you, too."

Lotus's lids drifted shut as she enjoyed the tingling sensation of me kissing *the* spot on the nape that always drove her wild. She ran her hands over my face as the air trapped between us grew thicker. Between the sweet aroma of her perfume and the feeling of her smooth skin against my fingertips, I didn't know which experience I enjoyed more.

"Turn around." I growled in her ear.

I ripped her silk robe off before cupping her full breasts through her bra. I quickly freed them before massaging and kneading her nipples between my index and middle fingers. Lotus clenched her thighs together just as I pulled her panties to the side and bent her over the couch. I dropped to my knees and spread her pussy lips to eat her from behind. I kept each stroke of my tongue deliberately slow, savoring the taste I'd craved while in her absence.

"Mmmm," she purred, getting wetter by the second.

I spun her around and kissed up her bare stomach until I'd made my way back up to her lips. Lotus dropped to her knees and pulled my pants down with her before taking my length into her warm mouth to get my shit nice and wet. I stroked her jawline as she slid my dick in and out, pushing out jagged breaths as she picked up the pace.

I frowned while biting down on my bottom lip. "Shit."

Lotus ran her long fingernails up and down my brown thighs, and I knew we were too far gone to stop. There was no more pretending and no turning back. I wanted more than her heart. I *had* to have every piece of her. I pulled Lotus to her feet and flipped her back around to face the couch before bending her over. She dug her nails into the fabric as my hard dick pushed past her walls.

"Ahh!" she screamed, sharply sucking in a breath.

I slapped my hand over her mouth to keep her quiet. It was clear we'd both forgotten we were in the house of the Lord. "Shh! Don't you make another fuckin' sound, or I'll stop."

She looked over her left shoulder at me, smiling devilishly. I'd always been dominant in the bedroom. It only made my dick harder when she submitted to me. I roughly mashed my lips against hers to stifle her moans.

Lotus's breast jiggled inside my right hand as I locked the other around her nape. I pounded her pussy harder, bending her further over the couch. She belted out a stifled moan while biting into the throw pillow.

"Mmmm, shit! Yes! Right there, Psalm! Keep it right there!"

Her lipstick smeared instantly. I kept my stroke steady. With each thrust, another one of her curls sweated out. I found pleasure in watching her body quake as she came. She was cumming, orgasming, falling, rising, and falling again. She'd never been wetter. To me, *that's* what love felt like. Lotus violently threw her ass back, slapping against my thighs as she rode the most dangerous wave of her life. My chest heaved in and out as I gripped her hips tighter. We were both sweating and panting like animals as I thrust inside her, seconds from the release of a lifetime.

"Shit." He groaned.

"Don't pull out, baby! I want your baby, Psalm!" she moaned while locking her arms around my waist to keep me buried inside her.

As soon as I inhaled, my body released. My knees turned to water as my body jerked and shook. Before I had a chance to recover, there was a loud boom against the other side of the door.

"Lotus? Psalm? What the fuck is going on in there?" Kareem yelled before banging his fist against the door again.

Her lipstick was smeared. My pants were down. And my best friend was going crazy on the other side of the door.

"Open this fuckin' door right now!" Kareem yelled, banging harder.

"*Fuck!*" I whispered as he fumbled to pull his pants up from around his ankles. Our nightmare had suddenly become a reality.

I quickly pulled away from Lotus, redressing promptly while she stared me down.

"What are you doing?" I asked through gritted teeth. "Put your clothes on, now! Don't you hear him banging?"

"I'm not running anymore, Psalm. I'm done. This shit stops here. *All* of it," she confirmed while pulling on her robe and tying it tightly around her waist.

Rage burned in my eyes as I levied a glare her way. I flinched when the door rattled again at the sound of Kareem's fist on the other side. Lotus walked over to unlock the door before I could stop her. When it swung open, Kareem was huffing and puffing as beads of sweat danced down his forehead. His chest heaved in and out as his eyes searched Lotus's for answers.

"What the fuck is going on? What took you so long to open the door, and where is Psalm?" he roared.

She twisted her neck in my direction. "He's right over there."

Kareem barged past her, marching into the suite as if he owned it. He came to a crashing halt when his eyes met mine. He whipped his neck back at Lotus. "I'm only going to ask you both this question one fuckin' time. What the fuck is going on between you two? I *know* there's something," he accused, baring his teeth.

Neither of us said a word. It wasn't like the thought of Kareem finding out about Lotus and me hadn't crossed my mind, but I was at a loss for words when the moment arrived. I suppose the silence hanging between us was answer enough.

"Y'know, I was gon' save this for my vows, but since it doesn't look like we're gonna get to that today, I'll tell you now," Kareem explained.

Lotus parted her lips. "Kareem, I—"

His hand waved her silent while he shook his head back and forth. "My heart was frozen when I got back to the States from my deployment. I was so fucked up that I'd given up on finding love and even loving myself. Adjusting back to being a civilian was hard. It was so hard that I tried to take my life behind it. After my failed attempt, I ran into the most beautiful angel I'd ever seen while I was making groceries. It was aisle seven with the cereal and shit. I forget a lot, but I'll never forget that moment. That was the moment I said to myself, '*Damn, God gotta be lookin' out for a nigga to bring her into my life.*' You were gorgeous and witty. I fell in love with you before I pulled out of the parking lot. You were the only woman on earth who'd been able to thaw my heart and keep it beating up until now."

She parted her lips to speak again. "Kareem, I'm—"

"Was any of it real?" he asked, cutting her off.

He directed his attention to me before she could answer. A hopeless expression hung on my face. "How could you do this to me, man? Me! You were supposed to be my best friend! My brother!"

"Kareem, listen, I'm—"

"Enough with the lies, Psalm! He knows! It's over! This shit has gone on long enough as it is! He needs to hear the truth! He deserves that much!" Lotus interjected.

"If he won't tell me, then you do it," Kareem replied.

She huffed as she kept her arms pinned to her chest. "Kareem, what Psalm and I have is... well, it's complicated. It's complicated, and it's special. It's a rollercoaster and a train wreck all wrapped into one. It never should've gone on this long without you knowing, but now you do," Lotus confessed.

As soon as the words fell off her tongue, everything inside me lit up like lights in Times Square on New Year's Eve. We were free. We were *finally* free.

Kareem's face squinted with confusion. "So, this is deeper than fucking? Y-you *love* him?"

"I do. I always have, and I'll never stop," she admitted.

"And what about you? What do you have to say for yourself? You love her back?" Kareem asked me.

Lotus shot her eyes over to me. Everyone was looking to me for answers I didn't know I had. My hands ran down my face repeatedly as if I was stuck in a trance. We were finally standing in the middle of our moment of truth, and I was so frozen I may as well have been a statue.

My broad chest deflated with a sigh. "I do."

"How long has this been going on?" Kareem probed.

"We met over a year ago at a holiday party and dated for a couple of months until I ghosted her after your suicide attempt," I explained.

Kareem sucked his teeth. "I can't fuckin' believe this shit!"

"I tried to stay away from her, man! I swear to God I did! For you! I wanted you to be happy even if it meant I never could be, but I love her, man. I worship the fuckin' ground she walks on, but seeing you lying in that hospital bed being watched like a hawk was hard on me and your parents. You didn't want to do the treatment programs or take any medication. You wanted to give up, and we refused to let you! So, you remember when I told you whatever we had to do to make sure you stayed here with us, we'd do it? I was desperate to find anything to keep you here, so I asked Lotus to do the unthinkable. It was the worst mistake I ever made in my life. I'm sorry I put you in the middle of it. I'm sorry I put both of you in the middle of it. I just wanted everyone to win, me included. And this was the only way I knew how to do it."

"I guess the signs were always there. I just got good at ignoring them. But there are some things even I can't ignore. Like the scent of the cologne he's been wearing since high school that's always stuck in your clothes, or the pair of spare panties you keep in your glove compartment for when you meet with him on short notice," he revealed as his voice trailed off.

Lotus's brows raised toward her hairline. "*You knew?*"

"I'd always had a lingering suspicion that there was more going on between you two than either of you would admit, but I always pushed the paranoia to the back of my mind because of how you treated each other. But now that the proof is staring me in the face, I'd be a fool to ignore it."

"It was *never* personal, Kareem," Lotus assured him.

"You sure about that? Because it sure as fuck feels that way. I feel like the biggest joke in town right now! I could feel it in my bones something wasn't right. I even came to you about it, and you tried to throw me off your trail by making me feel crazy and saying it was the meds! Why the fuck would you hook me up with a bitch you *knew* you had feelings for?"

"To save your goddamn life! I wanted to keep you here! We all did! Me, your mom, your dad! All of us!" I confessed.

Every muscle in Kareem's body seemed to tighten as he stood there, soaking in the news. Not only had his best friend and his bride betrayed him, but his parents were in on it, too. Heat burned his cheeks as he turned his attention back to Lotus.

"My parents have money, and so does Psalm. Did... did they fuckin' pay you to be with me?" Kareem probed.

Lotus sunk her teeth into her bottom lip while diverting her eyes to the fuzzy slippers covering her feet. "Yes," she revealed.

His brow creased. "How much?"

"C'mon, Reem. Let it go, aight? It's not important," I butted in.

Kareem shot me a menacing glare. "Nigga, fuck you! How much, Lotus?"

"One million at first, and then there's another five million after we're married," she answered.

A deep frown creased his brow. "*Five million dollars?*" he repeated in disbelief. "That's all my fuckin' life is worth to you?" he quizzed in disgust.

"I'm sorry you had to find out like this, Reem. I swear to God I never meant to hurt you like this," I confessed.

Kareem scoffed, brushing off his comment. "All I ever wanted to be was loved, get the respect I deserve, and be treated like the man I was raised to be by my peers and my family, but I guess there are some things money just can't fuckin' buy."

"As fucked up as it sounds, you gotta know everything we did was *all* for you."

"Get the fuck outta here with that shit! You were supposed to be my brother! Blood couldn't make us any closer!"

"I'm still your brother!" I declared while smacking my palm against the center of my chest.

Hot, vengeful tears pooled in the corners of Kareem's eyes as he lunged at Lotus. "And you! You were supposed to be my wife!" he roared.

She scrambled backward, and I stepped in front of her. "Get away from her!" I ordered, outstretching my arms to keep Kareem from getting to her.

Heat spread across his chest as he smacked my hands away. "Fuck you, Psalm!" he exploded. "Fuck you! Fuck her! Fuck my parents! Fuck all this shit!"

Suddenly, there was a knock on the door before Lotus's cousin barged inside. "What the *hell* is going on down here?" Tiffany hissed while looking around at the three of us.

Kareem drew in a frustrated breath. "Go back upstairs and tell everybody the wedding is off! If they have questions, tell them to mind their fuckin' business!"

Tiffany's brows creased. "*What?*"

"Please go, Tiff," Lotus huffed, eyeing her closely.

"Fine! I'll make the announcement, but it's not like they can't hear y'all yelling from upstairs! I suggest that whatever the three of you have going on, you either squash it or take that shit outside. This is the house of the goddamn lord!" she huffed.

As soon as Tiffany left, Kareem brought his lips close to Lotus's. Her eyes bore into his soul, only to see there wasn't a damn thing there. All that remained was the glaring anger and unbearable pain pouring from his sad brown eyes.

"I wish it didn't have to be like this," he stated as tears slid down his face. "Why the *fuck* couldn't you love me past my flaws the way that I loved you past yours, Lo?"

She wagged her head. "You can find love again with someone else, Kareem, someone whose heart doesn't already belong to someone else. I *want* you to find someone who truly loves you back," I emphasized.

"That was supposed to be you! Don't you get that? I loved you with everything I had left in me, Lo! I know I'm not perfect, but I thought you were the one person who saw past my baggage and my bullshit. I-I thought you loved me to my core."

"Kareem, I'm sorry, okay? I'm so sorry. I tried to tell you so many times, but I want to be with Psalm. I just don't love you *the way I love him*."

He glared at me for a few fleeting seconds without blinking. There was nothing behind his eyes, no soul, no remorse, no nothing.

"I knew there'd come a time when I had to use this again. Never in a million years did I think it would be because of *you*," Kareem told me as he pulled back his tuxedo jacket and brandished the handgun secured on his hip.

I anchored my gaze to his weapon as my eyes bulged with terror. I remained rooted in front of Lotus, shielding her body with my own. "Yo, what the fuck, Kareem? Whatever you're thinking right now, I promise you, you don't want to do it."

"K-Kareem, l-listen to him. P-lease p-put the gun d-down," Lotus stuttered.

Kareem aimed the gun at us while wagging his head from left to right. "I see how everyone looks at me like I'm half a fuckin' man. Like I'm broken and shit. I expected better from you, nigga. I expected better from both of you! And all you did was flaunt your money around to the highest bidder, so I could be babysat and wouldn't fucking kill myself! And you! So easily bought while he pulled your strings like a goddamn puppet! He doesn't love you! He doesn't give a fuck about your ass!" Kareem hissed, spewing his insults at her.

"Yes, he does!" she yelled.

"He only loves himself! Are you that dick dizzy that you can't fuckin' see he practically pimped you out to me? He sold you to the highest bidder, and your dumb ass let him. Does that sound like something someone would do if they *truly* loved you, Lotus? Huh?"

The suite fell silent while Kareem's chest rattled with every exhale. He was furious. As badly as Lotus wanted the truth to come out, in Kareem's eyes, he'd been made to look like a fool, a charity case, even.

"I had plans for us, baby. So many fuckin' plans. You were supposed to be my wife and have my babies. Both of you mothafuckas deserve to die for what you did to me!" he yelled, repositioning his aim to the center of my chest.

Lotus screamed, crouching behind me. "Oh my God, please don't! I'm pregnant!" she shouted.

I watched Kareem's eyes bulge in surprise. "Y-you're what?"

"I'm p-pregnant," Lotus repeated.

"Don't tell me it's..." he asked, letting his voice trail off before finishing his sentence.

Lotus slowly wagged her head. "It's Psalm's."

"How can you be so sure? We made love like a week ago!"

The loaded gun in his hand was my first concern, so I interjected. "Listen to me, Kareem! Look at me and fuckin' listen! I'll leave right now if you want me to. I swear to God I'll drop everything right now and go if that's what you want! Just please don't do this shit!" I pleaded.

Kareem scoffed. "Leaving is the least you could do, you fuckin' coward."

"Psalm, no!" Lotus yelled, tugging at my arm.

I shook my head while raising my hands in surrender. "Lotus, I'm sorry. Kareem put the gun down, and I'm out. I'm gone. You'll never have to see me again."

"Put the gun down, and you gone, huh? So, you'd just break her heart like that and leave like a thief in the night? For me?"

"Yes, for you! I did all of this for you! I know you can't see that shit right now, but I did!"

"For me, huh?"

"Yeah, for you!"

"Remind me again which part you did for me, nigga. Was it fuckin' my fiancée behind my back or paying her to date me in the mothafuckin' first place?"

I released an exasperated sigh. I was defeated. Only I knew the truth behind my intentions. I didn't mind standing ten toes down and taking the blame for making all the wrong decisions surrounding the three of us. All I wanted to do was find a solution to the problem. If leaving the church or even NOLA for good fixed it, then that's what I would do.

"What do you want me to do? Tell me, and I'll do it!"

Kareem shook his head. "Nah, you know what I want you to do? Tell me what you want since you are the mothafucka who gets everything he wants, right? Do you want to be with her? Tell me the truth, nigga!"

"All I want is for you to put down the gun. I don't want to see you go out like this. Neither of us do."

Kareem's nostrils flared as he swiped away the tears clouding his view. "You should've just let me die, man." He sobbed, tears garbling his words. "Because without you, I ain't got shit left to lose."

"What you mean? I'm right here, man. All I need you to do is put the gun down, Reem, please, yo."

"Please listen to him, Kareem," Lotus pleaded while holding onto my waist from behind.

Kareem let out a silent chuckle. "Y'know, I'm gettin' real sick and fuckin' tired of this! From the moment I stepped foot back in the States, I've been treated like either a hero or a plague. You mothafuckas don't know what it's like to take a life! You don't know the pieces of myself I lost over there that I'll *never* get back! You don't know shit! You think it'll hurt me to pull this trigger, huh? Do you? I've killed for less!"

My abs tightened with knots as fear clawed at my throat. Never in a million years did I imagine I'd be staring down the barrel of a gun on my best friend's wedding day. The lesser parts of me hoped Kareem would accept the truth and allow her to move on with the man she truly loved, even if it *was* his best friend. But I knew him too well. His pride would never let him go out like that.

In the blink of an eye, Kareem forcefully shoved me into a wall before latching his calloused hands around Lotus's throat.

"Look at me!" he screamed, forcing her to look into his dark eyes as he held the gun to her chest.

She clawed her nails into his biceps. "Kareem, please," she whispered, gasping for her next breath.

"Kareem, no!" I roared, pulling myself back up to my feet. I lunged at Kareem to knock him off her, but I was too late.

POW!

My eyes ballooned as I watched Lotus's body fall to the ground. I broke into a run to be at her side. I reached out to bundle her in my arms and cradle her like a glass egg. My vision became watery as I put pressure on the gunshot wound to her chest to stop the blood from pouring out.

"Look what you did! Look what the fuck you did!" I thundered as a cry rose within me.

Kareem lifted his shoulder in a half-shrug. "At least now you both know how it feels to have a broken heart."

"Somebody help! Somebody call nine-one-one! Please!" I roared frantically while cradling Lotus's body and rocking her from side to side.

"Just remember, you did this shit, Psalm! All this is on you! You wanted to have your fuckin' cake and eat it too, and now look! Look at her!"

I broke eye contact with him and let my gaze fall over Lotus's lifeless body. My heart shattered as a spine-shuddering sob built up in the back of my throat. Tears burned at the borders of my eyes. All I wanted to do was make the pain go away like a bad dream, yet I was stuck in the middle of my worst nightmare.

"Are you happy now? Is this what you wanted? Huh? Is it?" I shouted as spit flew from the corners of my mouth.

"Just know I always loved you, man. You were more than my best friend, P. You were my brother," Kareem stated while aiming his gun at my chest.

My eyes bored through Kareem in silence. The only thing I could hear was the loud thumping of my accelerated heartbeat inside my chest. There was no more pleading, begging, or reasoning with him. His mind was made up, and my fate had been signed and sealed.

I dipped my chin out of respect. "I love you, too."

Kareem pulled the trigger. Everything went black the moment I felt the bullet pierce my flesh.

POW!

EIGHT

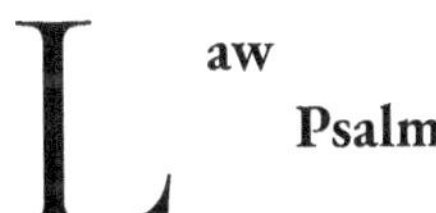

"Wake up, Psalm! Wake up! Yo, wake up!"

I shot up in a cold sweat. My eyes refocused to see Kareem hovering over me with a concerned expression on his face. I sized him up. He was clad in his custom-fitted black tuxedo and red bottom loafers. He had his bowtie in one hand and a glass of whiskey on ice in the other.

"What the fuck?" I mumbled, my chest tight with panic.

Sweat poured down my body, dampening my dress shirt. *None of it was real.* Yet, there was a quaking deep beneath my ribs I couldn't shake.

"Yo, you good?"

"I-I don't know. I must've nodded off back here somehow. What the fuck was in that drink?" I inquired, eyes darting to the half-filled highball glass of whiskey.

"Guess that's what you get for gettin' buzzed in a church," Kareem joked.

I wiped the trail of sweat from my hairline. "Y-yeah."

"You sure you aight? Because I know that look."

"What look?"

"You look like you've seen a ghost."

It was the smoothness of his eerie words that sent an unsettling chill down my spine. My nightmare had provided me with the depressing clarity that everything *always* came to the light, no matter how deep our secrets were buried. Everything we'd fought so hard to keep quiet wouldn't matter if Lotus was dead. Seeing the life leave Lotus's body ignited a flame of loss in my chest. I couldn't stand the emptiness of the cavity in my ribs would be without her. Her heart needed to keep beating so that mine would too.

I wagged my head. "You got any aspirin or something? My fuckin' head is throbbin'."

"I think there may be some in the bathroom. I'll get it for you."

"Yeah, thanks."

Kareem came back a few minutes later and handed me two pills. I quickly tossed them in my mouth before picking up the glass on the table next to me and slinging the rest of the dark liquor down the back of my throat. "Pour up another one," I instructed him. Kareem walked over to the bottle and poured me another shot. He passed it back, and I held my glass in the air while forcing a smile. "Here's to you on your... day."

I swallowed the melon-sized lump in my throat before tossing back the shot. I needed all the liquid courage I could get if I was going to stop my best friend's wedding. Kareem lifted his glass to his lips when a knock sounded on the other side of the door. He set his glass down to go see who it was. I stood, and all the blood rushed to my head, making it thump like an HBCU marching band. I shook my hands out in front of me before walking to the bathroom to splash some cold water on my face. I'd hoped the chill would help me decipher reality from make-believe. After a few minutes, I walked back over to Kareem and gave him a once-over. His haircut and outfit were fresh. He was almost completely dressed except for the unfastened bowtie hanging around his neck. Yet, all the color had been leeched from his face as a look of uncertainty claimed his expression.

"There's a problem."

"What's up, man? Don't tell me you got a case of cold feet."

"It's not me," he said, throwing his shot back.

"Huh? What's going on?"

"Tiffany just came up here again."

"*Who*?"

"Lotus's cousin. She's the matron of honor. I don't know what to do, man. She said Lotus *still* isn't ready. She won't come out of the suite. You don't think she wants to call off the wedding, do you?"

The mere mention of her name hollowed out my stomach. I slowly wagged my head. My newfound conscience taunted me over just how far I'd let things go and how much worse shit could get. *This is your chance to tell the truth, Psalm.* It was judgment day, and I was standing smack in the middle of my moment of truth. There were a million words trying to skydive off my tongue, and yet, nothing would come out. I knew better than to say, *I'm sorry* or *My bad*. What I'd done to my best friend was deeper than that, but there was no Hallmark card for our particular situation. I parted my lips to speak, but before sound could escape, Kareem interjected with a request.

"Can you please go back down there and see what's going on?"

My brows compressed over my eyes. "*Back*?"

"The wedding was supposed to start over an hour ago, Psalm. You already went down there thirty minutes ago."

"I did?"

Kareem gave me a hard stare. "Are you all here today, nigga? C'mon, P. You're my best man. You can't let this shit fall apart on me at the last minute. There are too many people out there that I *refuse* to let down."

I knew image was everything, especially to someone with parents like Kareem's. "I'll go," I said gallantly.

Kareem patted my shoulder. "Thanks, P. You know I'll return the favor one day if you're ever in my shoes."

I exited the back room and sauntered toward the other side of the church where Lotus and her bridesmaids were supposed to have been getting ready. The further I walked, the more I felt myself retracing my footsteps. What the hell had happened to me? I still felt woozy but coherent enough to put one foot in front of the other until I arrived in front of the door. I knocked before retracting a few steps.

"What are you doing back here?" Tiffany hissed with a frown while only cracking the door a sliver.

I cleared my throat. "I came to see what the holdup is."

"There's no holdup anymore. Tell Kareem she's *finally* ready to walk down the aisle," she confirmed before slamming the door in my face.

"Fuck," I hissed.

I slowly walked back to where I'd left Kareem to deliver the news. If I was the real man I'd always proclaimed myself to be, why the *hell* was I still hiding behind my lies? Real men didn't cower behind contracts and agreements. They *definitely* didn't steal their best friend's girls and impregnate them. They didn't break the hearts of the people they claimed to love. They protected them at all costs. They told the truth and suffered whatever consequences followed. It was at that moment that I decided I didn't care what I had to do. I was going to stop Lotus from marrying Kareem, even if it meant the end of our friendship. I'd wash my hands of my sins later.

———

A layer of icy sweat sat on my skin as I stood beside Kareem at the altar, watching, waiting for Lotus to emerge. The pills he'd given me still hadn't kicked in. My head hurt so bad my damn vision had started to blur. Her cousin Tiffany came down first. She had a face I recognized but couldn't place. Maybe if I had more time or more desire to, I would've thought about it more, but I didn't. The only person I wanted to see was Lotus. I was dying to lay eyes on her. The song started, and the crowd stood in anticipation, ready to welcome her in. I'd never known how mournful a love song could sound until that very moment. Everyone in the crowd instantly became a blur of faces the moment I pinned my eyes on the bride. I couldn't unfreeze my face as the radiant angel inched up the aisle closer toward him, toward *us*. Lotus was the most beautiful bride I'd ever seen. Her steps minced the length of the aisle painfully slow, biding her time and stretching the seconds out as thinly as possible. I could tell by the telltale trembling of her hands she didn't want to marry him. She wanted me to save her. She was all but begging me to.

Sweat puddled in my palms as I caught Kareem's expression from the corner of my eye. I watched his reaction for a sign of uncertainty, but his expression was unreadable. A single tear slipped down her veiled cheek as she stood before Kareem. I stood there, staring a hole in the side of her face, devastated that she wouldn't even look at me.

The officiant started, and the three of us turned our attention to him. "Dearly beloved, we are gathered here today amongst friends and family of the bride and groom. Today is a day of love, happiness, and fellowship as we celebrate the union of the happy couple."

After a prayer and a few more words from the Bible, he turned to the guests. "If anyone objects to this union, speak now or forever hold your peace."

I looked out into the crowd of guests, all hanging onto their silence and baiting their breath while waiting for the ceremony to continue. *It's now or fuckin' never, nigga.*

Emotion swelled at the back of my tongue as I parted my lips. "Kareem," I called out, voice low. "I'm sorry, but I *can't* let you marry her."

He snapped his eyes at me. "*What*? Why not?"

I sighed. "Because somewhere along the way, she carved her name into my chest, and now I can't let her go, Reem, not even to you."

All the color drained from Kareem's warm brown face as he turned to Lotus to confirm or deny. "I-is this true?"

She nodded slowly before moving to stand by my side. "Psalm was always supposed to be standing where you are."

Kareem scoffed before taking a few steps back away from the both of us. "Are you fuckin' serious right now?"

I raised my palms to him, feeling the sweat pour down the back of my neck. "Hear me out."

"I don't wanna hear you out, nigga! This is my wedding day!" Kareem barked.

His anger was warranted, expected even. "Please, Reem. It wasn't supposed to be like this."

"Then what the fuck was it supposed to be like? Because from any angle you spin it, this shit is fucked up!"

"We met a couple months before your suicide attempt. It was the happiest I'd been in a long time. But when you tried t-to take your life, I... didn't know what to do. You wouldn't talk to anyone about anything. You were so emotionally scarred that we knew you needed someone to love you through your pain, so I asked Lotus to do the *unthinkable*. I asked her to—"

"Don't say it!" he cut me off.

I lowered my gaze. "I'm sorry."

Lotus interjected with her own apology. "I'm sorry too, Kareem."

"You two have been fucking behind my back this entire time? Even before I met you?" he questioned.

I nodded. "Yes. It was the *worst* mistake I ever made in my life. I'm sorry I put you in the middle of it. I'm sorry I put *both* of you in the middle of it. I just wanted everyone to win, me included. And this was the only way I knew how to do it," I said, taking full responsibility and leaving his parents out of it.

If my confession had taught me anything, it was that taking care of someone because you loved them and taking care of them because you wanted them to love themselves were two different things.

"Why, P? Why would you do this to me? To her?"

"I lied to her," I confessed. "I lied to you. I *lied*, okay? I lied because lies are more filling than the truth, especially when you know the person you're deceiving is starving. If I could go back, I would do everything differently. But I guess that's why they say hindsight is twenty-twenty."

"Was any of it real?"

Lotus slowly wagged her head without letting a sound drip from her lips.

"Look at me, Lo," Kareem demanded. "Do you wanna be with him? Hm? You love him?"

"I do, Kareem. I'm sorry. Psalm is right. We never should've let things get *this* far," she said, outstretching her arms while looking to her left and right.

Kareem wagged his head. His expression was a mask as he parted his lips. "For years, I've been holding onto this unbearable rage, this loud silence echoing inside the hollowest parts of me, and I wanna let it go. I *need* to before it finishes eating away at the last few pieces left of me," he said, tongue tiptoeing around the words.

"Kareem, what are you talking about?"

"I fell in love when I was overseas," he revealed.

"*What*? Y-you never mentioned that before."

"I couldn't. It was too precious, too delicate for just anyone's ears. I'd never been connected to another human being like that before. To be honest, it was scary. It was like our hearts had known each other for another lifetime. Hearing you talk about Lotus lets me know you understand the feeling. You both do."

"Where is she?" Lotus asked. "Why haven't you been with her instead of me this time?"

"*He's* dead," Kareem corrected and informed her at the same time. "The love of my life died in my arms the day of the accident."

"Oh my God!" his mother screamed.

"Oh, shit," Lotus mumbled in shock.

My brows rose in a slow arch as breath snagged in my throat. "Hold up. Reem, are you saying you're…"

"I'm bisexual, Psalm."

I blinked rapidly as a fresh sweat sprang from my pores. "Why didn't you ever say anything?"

He cut me a glare. "You don't have to touch a hot stove to know you'll get burned if you do."

"You could've told me."

"I couldn't tell anybody. Ain't you ever heard of don't ask, don't tell? Besides, be real. Who the fuck wanted to hear that shit comin' from me? My father is a general!" he yelled, pointing to his father frozen on the front pew a few feet away.

"You could've told me," I assured him.

Kareem wagged his head back and forth as tears sparkled in his eyes. "You've never had to try to be normal, Psalm. You just were. But for me, that shit wasn't easy. I hid the real me from all of you for so long because I never wanted anyone to see the suffering I endure *every day*." He stopped and swallowed. "I'd become so good at smiling through the pain. You think you're a good liar? I'm the king of make-believe. It's hard not to be fooled by what you see when you look at me," he confessed.

"That's enough!" Kareem's father yelled before storming down the aisle.

His mother rose to her feet soon after. She looked at Kareem with sorrow and remorse in her eyes. "I'm *so* sorry, baby. This is all just too much for him right now," she apologized before chasing after her husband.

Kareem's sad eyes glittered with tears as he watched his parents turn their backs on him.

"I'm sorry about that... about them," I told him.

He wagged his head before smearing the tears from his cheeks. "I'd never seen him look prouder of me the day I graduated from basic training. How could I tell him I'd fallen in love with another man? I knew he'd never look at me the same way again, and today, he proved me right."

"H-how long have you known?" Lotus questioned.

"Aaron was the first and only man I'd ever been with. It was like we were two sides of the same coin. Aaron was an Aries like me, and he even liked anime just as much as me, if not more. He lived behind the same invisible wall as I did, but somehow, he always made me feel like I was the biggest, brightest star in the desert night sky. I never thought I'd find someone who saw through my hard exterior straight to my chaos, but then I met him. And he didn't run when he saw my pain. He stayed. He stayed, and he nurtured it. When you're a soldier, you're taught that strength is your greatest attribute. I believed that until Aaron died. That's when I learned that iron will was the greater than strength. Without it, I never would've made it out of that combat zone. I wanted to die with him, but I didn't because as much as I loved him, I knew I couldn't let you down. I couldn't let anybody down."

"Why'd you date me and ask me to marry you if you knew you wanted to be with a man?" Lotus inquired.

"I don't want to be with just *any* man, Lotus. The man I wanted to be with is dead. Allowing myself to feel anything for another person was a hard line I thought I'd never cross again, and then I met you. You changed my life in the best way. I thought you were the remedy to my sadness because of the time you came into my life. Now I'm realizing just how wrong I've been. I promised him I'd never let anything life threw my way break me, no matter how hard it tried or how dark it got. I promised him I'd try, but now I know that this... this isn't the path any of us need or want to go down."

Lotus tilted her head to the side. "So, you're fine with calling this off and walking away?"

"One of the biggest lessons that stuck with me after losing Aaron was that the world doesn't stop turning for any of us. I don't wanna waste any more time not searching for the right something or someone waiting for me out there."

Kareem's revelation made me realize that our secrets were only a tangled thread of memories we wished we could forget. I couldn't have been prouder of him for standing on his truth. With all that had been revealed, I refrained from bringing up the fact that Lotus was pregnant. We'd spilled enough tea to last a lifetime.

"Thank you for sharing your truth, and fuck apologizing to anybody for it. You gotta live your life for you, Reem. Moving forward, you make the decisions that are gonna be best for you."

I reached out to dap him up. He looked down at my hand before slapping his palm against mine and pulling me into a hug. "I love you, man."

"I love you, too, Reem," I told him before pulling away and turning my attention to Lotus. "And you... Lotus, I am so in love with you."

We'd all been thrown for a loop, but Kareem had proven that his rock bottom was nothing but a base for him to rebuild his life brick by brick. Now that the truth was out, he was free to live the way he always wanted and on his own terms. It was time I did the same.

Her breath hitched as I reached out to hold her palms in mine. "I know I've done a lot of fucked up shit to you in the name of love, and because of it, I realize I may never be able to fully repair the damage I've done to your heart. And the only thing I can think of to make things right is to offer you mine in exchange. All you have to do is say yes," I proposed before sanity kicked in and talked my ass out of it.

NINE

I n Exchange
  Lotus

The moment I'd been waiting for what felt like my entire life for had *finally* arrived. I'd been in love with Psalm Baptiste for what felt like a million years. My insides sparked with color whenever he looked at me. Every bone in my body *knew* he was the one. He may have been deeply flawed, but in my eyes, there was no one more perfect for me. I closed my eyes, fully submerged in the special moment, and instantly saw hues of blue and purple exploding through my head. I didn't know what had come over him, but I was grateful for his change of heart. I'd found the man capable of giving me everything I deserved, and I was ready to give it back tenfold. My eyes were filled with tears when my lashes flipped open.

"Yes," I whispered.

"Yes?" Psalm asked, brows raised toward the sweat beads building on his hairline.

"My answer is yes. It will *always* be yes for you, Psalm Baptiste," I vowed as I crushed my body into his.

"You're such a beautiful bride," he whispered in my ear before his lips gently brushed against my forehead.

I could smell the transfer of his cologne on my skin. I smiled more genuinely than I had in what felt like forever. "So, what happens now?"

Psalm turned toward the officiant. "Can you marry us right here, right now?" he asked before swinging his neck in. Kareem's direction. "If it's okay with you."

"I can't stand in your way, Psalm. I've never been able to," Kareem replied before stepping aside.

The officiant cleared his throat. "Well then, for those of you who are left, we are *still* gathered here today to officially join two hearts that we've learned have long since been intertwined. Today's ceremony is a stamp and a shiny, red bow on a union preordained by the most high himself. With that being said, I will move straight to the vows if that's alright with the bride and the *new* groom."

"I'm good with that," Psalm agreed.

I nodded eagerly. Suddenly, the two words I'd dreaded saying all day couldn't come out of my mouth fast enough. "Me too."

My ears couldn't wait to hear him vow to love, honor, and obey me and *never* let me go again.

"Lotus, I'll start with you. Please repeat after me. I, Lotus."

"I, Lotus."

"Take you, Psalm, to be my husband, to have and to hold, for better or for worse, in sickness and in health, for as long as we both shall live."

I repeated the words clearly after the officiant as my hand gently swept the side of Psalm's warm cheek. "I love you *so* much."

Psalm shot me a lopsided grin. "I l-love y-you, too," he slurred as his eyes glazed over.

"Baby, are you okay?"

"Mmhm. I'm fine."

"You're sweating a lot."

"I-I think... something's wrong, Lo—" he stuttered before his body thudded to the floor.

. . .

An explosion of screams sounded off amongst the guests, Tiffany and I included. I screamed a cry as I fell to my knees, cradling his head in my lap. Tiffany was right by my side, with terror filling her eyes.

"No! Psalm? Psalm! Wake up! Wake up, baby! Wake up! There's no way you can leave me like this, baby!" I pleaded while shaking him with all my might. "Go get help, Tiff! Call 9-1-1!"

———

I sat in the waiting room, leg shaking underneath my wedding dress, as Tiffany held my trembling hands. I hardly spoke or even glanced her way for the first half hour we were there. I felt physically and emotionally exhausted. Without knowing if Psalm would live or die, I couldn't organize my thoughts around the fact that he'd gone from proposing to passing out in front of me. Kareem sat across from us. I didn't have the energy to speak, to apologize, to ask how he was feeling. With all the shock and trauma the day had already delivered, I didn't even know how I felt other than void. I figured it was best for all of us if I gave him time to digest all that had bubbled up.

"Why haven't they come back with any answers yet?" I finally asked.

"I'm sure as soon as they know something, we'll know something," she assured me while squeezing my hand.

I nodded before laying my head on her shoulder. She was the only reassurance I had. "This can't be how our love story ends, Tiff. It just can't," I whispered as another spine-shuddering sob built up inside me. She remained silent for a few seconds, allowing me the chance to speak up again. "I have to pee, but I don't wanna move."

"Girl, if you don't go to the bathroom. I'll let you know if anything happens while you're gone."

I sighed, knowing I only had a few minutes left, at best, before my bladder exploded. "Okay. I'll be right back."

I'd already scoped out the restroom, so I knew the exact direction I was headed. I caught a glimpse of my gloomy reflection in the mirror as I washed my hands. My bladder may have been empty, but I didn't feel any more relieved. My shoulders rose and fell with a quick sigh as I prepared to go back to the waiting area.

“I’m looking for the family of Psalm Baptiste,” I heard a male doctor call out as I made my way back to Tiffany.

My heart galloped in my chest as I raced toward him, dress catching under my heels along the way. Before I could part my lips to speak, Tiffany shot up with Kareem not far behind.

“Yes! That’s me! *I’m his wife*!” she exclaimed.

Her words made me rest on my heels, pausing momentarily before starting again. *Why the fuck would she say that?* By the time I approached them, the doctor started spilling vital information I didn’t want to miss, so I shut the hell up and stood there.

“Mrs. Baptiste, we found several traces of neurotoxic snake venom in your husband’s system.”

“*What*?” I snapped. “H-how?”

“He somehow ingested a potent amount.”

My heart stuttered. “You’re saying someone *poisoned* him?”

“You’re lucky the paramedics got him here when they did, or I’m afraid the consequences would have been fatal.”

“Is he going to be okay?” Kareem blurted out.

“We’re still monitoring him closely and running multiple tests, but with the proper treatment plan, we expect Mr. Baptiste to make a partial, if not full, recovery.”

“Oh, thank God,” Tiff replied, breathing a sigh of relief with her hand over her heart.

“Thank you so much, doctor. When can I see him?” I asked.

His brow creased as he snapped his eyes at Tiffany and then me. “The family can go in any time now. He’s in room 4155.”

“Thank you,” Tiffany assured him before he walked away.

My eyebrows crashed into the middle of my forehead. As happy as I was to hear Psalm would survive, I couldn’t shake how *off* Tiffany was acting. “What the fuck was that about, T?” I snapped immediately. “Why did you say that you were his wife?”

“Relax, Lo. You were gone. I didn’t want to miss the chance to get an update for you, okay? But thank God he’s okay, right? This is what we all wanted!”

I sized her up with a questioning brow. “*Mmhm*, right.”

“We should get in to see him.”

"Actually, I think you should wait out here."

"Why?"

"Because you're not his fucking wife, Tiffany! I am!" I barked.

What the fuck is this bitch not getting through her thick-ass skull?

Tiffany's perfectly arched brow curved with a dare before she flashed a smile full of knives. "Just when I thought you couldn't, there you go, landing on your feet *again*."

"Ain't that what I'm supposed to do?" I snapped, arranging my mouth in a sour line. "It's in our blood, remember?"

"It should've been you, y'know?" she muttered

There was a sudden uptick in my heartbeat. "*Excuse me?*"

"If only Psalm hadn't gotten in the way."

"What the *hell* are you talking about, Tiff? Are you—are you fucking with me right now?"

She sloped her head to the left. "You remember I told you about the first affair I had a long time ago?"

I scrunched up my features. "Yeah, so?"

Tiffany paused as another sinister smile spread its way across her lips. It didn't take long for me to put two and two together. *Psalm* was the man Tiffany had her first affair with, and something in her still hadn't let him go.

"Yeah. What's that shit Ray Jay says? *I hit it first*!" She cackled.

I swallowed the lump in my throat. "Y-you knew about Psalm and me this entire time! Why didn't you ever say anything?"

"What was there for me to say? What Psalm and I had happened long before you. He was my first slip-up two years into my marriage. I *thought* I'd curbed my craving for him after all these years, but after you told me about him and your sticky situation, I couldn't resist the urge to see him again, to breathe his air."

I scoffed. "Wow. I never noticed it before now, but you're *really* bat-shit crazy."

"I'm crazy about Psalm," she solidified. "We *both* know how mesmerizing he can be."

. . .

It felt like a truck had slammed into me head-on as I stared at her in silent disbelief. It was too unnerving to contemplate—the thought of her and Psalm together. I stood rooted in the existential shock of her revelation as her words replayed in my head like a broken record.

She'd been my confidant through it all.

She'd been there from the beginning.

She'd seen me rise, fall, and rise again.

And she'd been *plotting* against me the entire fucking time.

My own cousin had meddled with my life and played me for a fool. I'd been so blinded by my relationship with Psalm and Kareem that I couldn't see she'd wanted my life all along.

I bit my lip to contain a cry of rage. "How could you do this to me?"

Tiffany clicked her tongue. "Because everything is always about you, right? For *years,* I've been chasing the feeling he gave me. The closest I came to it was the nigga I was fuckin' with when Ellis caught me the second time, but it still wasn't quite the same. Then when I caught wind of all the mess you'd been stewing in and your surplus of niggas, I *knew* you didn't deserve him. You're a greedy *bitch*, Lo. You already had another nigga! But what do you do? You take, take, take!"

"Ain't that what you taught me to do?" I yelled, tears breaching my lids.

"I lost everything, and *you* gained the world."

"So, I don't deserve to be happy?"

"You weren't supposed to come up before me!"

The hurt of her words sliced right through me. Tiffany didn't give a *fuck* about me. She wanted to see me hurt, down bad, or worst of all, dead. Flashbacks of the past few months leading up to my wedding day started to echo in my thoughts.

"The snake venom in Psalm's system... that was you?"

"Hmm, *guilty*," Tiffany whispered. "I thought you'd drank the water I brought you until I saw him pass out at the altar."

I folded my arms across my chest as tears pumped out of my eyes. "And what about the notes? Were you behind that too?"

She snickered. "I warned you to your face, but you *still* didn't listen. So, I figured the notes would scare your ass straight. Yet here we are. I'm not even sure why I'm shocked. You're *Pretty Little Lotus* with her *perfect* little life and a face that earns her the keys to damn near anyone's heart. It's no wonder she meets the man of her dreams, gets not one, but *two* niggas to fall in love with her, a million dollars, *and* her dream restaurant. It's always been YOUR world. I'm just fucking living in it!"

All my words had been stolen from me. The word jealousy may as well have been written all over her face. I was sick over it.

"Don't be mad at me because I'm the main character of your life and mine! I paid you back tenfold for lookin' out for me! I haven't asked you for shit in years!" I thundered.

"You didn't have to! I'm your family! You didn't have to call. I was coming anyway. That's the way this shit has always worked, Lo! Who else was gonna be there to put you back together when your perfect little life was crumbling around you? Huh? Me! You've *always* been my burden!"

"*Bitch*, I'm your blessing, get it right! You are the definition of a *hater*. You don't know how to love. I've done nothing but try to take care of you, pay you back for lookin' out for me when we were younger. I gave you a fucking job at my restaurant! I let you move into my house after *you* let *your* greed blow up your life! But I guess it's my fault for thinking so highly of you when you *never* showed me you deserved it."

Tiffany tossed her hands up in surrender. "You know what, maybe you're right. Maybe I don't deserve your gratitude or your love. Maybe I'm just supposed to be *okay* with living in your fucking shadow! So, it's cool, you win. I'll leave."

My knuckles burned as my hands bunched into fists. "Yeah. I think that's a good fuckin' idea."

I was pregnant, and I *knew* it was wrong, but my emotions outweighed my reason. Tiffany's jealousy could've taken everything from me. I *wasn't* okay with that. Before I could stop myself, I saw my fist flying. *Whop!* I'd punched her, then retracted my fist. Her blood was bright red on my knuckles. No more tears would come to my eyes. In fact, all I saw from that moment forward was red. There was no sensible inner voice to listen to, to pump sense through my veins. The only voices speaking to me were spewing the toxic shit I wanted to hear. *Everything will feel clearer on the other side of your rage, Lotus. All you gotta do is get there.* I was possessed with rage, and I was going to beat my cousin's ass like she'd stolen something, which she had. At least she'd *tried* to.

"How could you do this shit to me, bitch?" I shouted before landing another demoralizing blow to the face, blackening the once blemish-free caramel-colored skin around her eye.

I knew I only had a small window of time before the nurses called for security and pulled me off her, but until then, I was going to beat her like a drum. With any luck, her shit would still be lumped up by the time my baby shower rolled around. I wanted her to think about me every time she looked in the mirror and remember she should've *never* fucked with me or *my* man.

It only took a few hits before Tiffany started to fight back. She got her initial lick back with a backslap to my lip. I instantly tasted the metallic tang of blood inside my mouth. *Fuckin' bitch.* Before I knew it, we were rolling around on the floor with our legs and arms intertwined as if we were deep in a game of Twister.

I grabbed a handful of her long hair and wound my hand around it before socking her in her button-nose one more time.

"You *don't* deserve him!" Tiffany hissed.

I already knew where Psalm's heart lay. I wasn't about to be on no Monica and Brandy's "The Boy is Mine" shit with her. All I wanted to do was beat her ass and see about *my* husband. I sledgehammered my fist at her, landing one last blow before I felt myself being pulled away by a source stronger than me. I couldn't fight against it. All I could do was surrender.

"That's enough, Lo. Let her go, that's enough." I heard Kareem's calming voice in my ear.

My body fell limp in his arms. Truth be told, I was *tired.* I shook my head as hot, vengeful tears raced down my cheeks. Seconds later, four security guards raced toward us.

"We got word of an altercation. What's going on?" one of the officers inquired.

"Arrest her! Arrest her right now before I fuckin' kill her!" I hissed, trying to break away from Kareem's arms.

He held strong without saying a word. His silence was the peace I'd been missing. I looked down at my stomach before shooting Kareem a worried look. "Find me a nurse, Kareem. I need someone to check on my baby," I announced.

EPILOGUE

L otus
Six months later.

"By the power vested in me and the Commonwealth of the Bahamas, I now pronounce you husband and wife. You may now kiss your bride," the officiant told us as the three of us stood under big sprays of greenery and vivid, colorful wildflowers.

Psalm stepped forward and cupped my face, stroking my tears away before he kissed me and then leaned down to kiss my pregnant stomach.

A mixture of soft, red, orange, and white rose petals were thrown at our feet as we strolled barefoot through the white sand. I cast my gaze onto the small crowd of witnesses as the wind tugged at my curls and carried the petals out to the sea. The cries of seagulls in the air, mixed with the soothing swish of the waves crashing into the rocks, were enough to bring a smile to my face. Yet, I was smiling for a different reason. We were expecting a healthy baby girl in a few months, and we were *finally* husband and wife. I closed my eyes and drew in a deep breath, smelling the salt water and sunscreen in the air. The ceremony was quick, but I didn't care. All I cared about was him. I was determined to soak up every bit of peace the day had to offer.

It took us going to hell and back for Psalm and me to end up together, but we made it. Psalm still had blank spots in his memory from that day, but with a vigorous treatment plan and therapy, he made the full recovery the doctors predicted he would. The beauty of it all was that we got each other, and Kareem got to decide how he wanted to present himself to the world moving forward. His relationship with his parents would never be the same, but at least he was free to be himself. Looking back on it all, it kind of made sense. Throughout our entire relationship, Kareem never fought any barrier I placed between us. I always thought it was his medication, but now I know it ran deeper than what met the eye.

When it was all said and done, everyone deserved some version of a happy ending with all the shit we'd been through. Everyone *except* for Tiffany's treacherous ass. Once Psalm found out what she'd done and recalled who she was, he moved mountains to ensure she was punished to the furthest extent for her obsession. Everyone had a past, including me. Plus, I knew there were two sides to every story. All I was focused on was nursing Psalm back to health. We had the rest of our lives to deal with the skeletons in our closet. I wasn't the only one who witnessed Tiffany's confession of drugging Psalm, and she was apprehended in the parking lot of the hospital by security and detained until the police arrived. Her ass was booked into jail, still wearing her bridesmaid's dress. Last I'd heard, she was facing two attempted murder charges *and* a sprinkle of blackmailing and stalking charges for the notes she'd sent to my restaurant. She could rot right where she was, as far as I was concerned.

If the past year had taught me anything, it was that it's the ones you love the most that you have to watch the closest. Her deceit forced me to examine the people around me, the ones I trusted the most. I hated what I saw. Because of it, that was a door that would remain closed for the rest of my life.

"What you thinkin' about, Mrs. Baptiste?" Psalm quizzed over the roaring crash of the waves at my back. "Better yet, what you stressin' 'bout?"

"What makes you think I'm stressin'?"

"There's a look you get. Trust me, I know it well," he said, being his typically charming self.

A light laugh fell past my lips. "You should."

"But for real, what's on your mind?"

"You and me, and how blessed we are," I answered as the warm ocean water slid over my feet.

"That we are," he agreed before kissing my cheek.

"I love you, Mrs. Baptiste."

"Mmm. I love it when you say that, baby," I purred.

"Oh yeah, *Mrs. Baptiste*?"

I cheesed. "Mmhm, and I love you, Mr. Baptiste."

We continued making footprints in the wet sand, hugging and talking while our photographer snapped dozens of candid photos behind us. I looked ahead at the hazy neighboring islands in the distance. Tiffany's hating ass was right about one thing: I *always* landed on my feet.

THE END

Afterword

A note from K.L. Hall.

Reader,

Thank you for reading "In Exchange: An Urban Thriller." If you've made it this far, I hope you'll consider telling me what you thought about the book in the form of a **five-star review and/or rating**. Don't hesitate to let me know what you'd like to see from me next! I thoroughly enjoy reading your thoughts and hearing from you as well! I'm always striving to attract new readers and retain current ones, and reviews are one of the easiest ways to attract readers. If you loved the book, tell a friend, and most importantly, let me know!

All my love,
K.L. Hall

About the Author

K.L. Hall is a national bestselling and award-winning author. As a serial storyteller, Hall has penned over three dozen titles in various genres—including African American urban fiction and romance, paranormal, children's books (as Kimberley M.), and non-fiction. Her fictional stories straddle the intersection of classic Urban and spell-binding Romance.

Highly Acclaimed Titles:

In the Arms of a Savage: (Peaked at #1 in Women's Fiction)

The Potomac Falls Series (Peaked at #1 and #2 in African American Erotica)

Sign up for my mailing list to stay updated with new releases, giveaways, sneak peeks, and more! Click this link: https://bit.ly/38RMpV5

Connect with me on social media:

Facebook: https://www.facebook.com/authorklhall

Twitter: https://twitter.com/authorklhall

Instagram: https://www.instagram.com/officialklhall/

Website: https://www.authorklhall.com

Other novels by K.L. Hall:

Diary of a Hood Princess 1-3

Rise of a Street King: The Justice Silva Story *(Spin-Off to the Diary of a Hood Princess series)*

Broken Condoms and Promises 1-3

In the Arms of a Savage 1-3

Built for a Savage: Blaze and Camille's Love Story *(Spin-Off to the In the Arms of a Savage Series)*

A Ruthle$$ Love Story 1-3

Fallin' for the Alpha of the Streets 1-2

The Most Savage of Them All: The Wolfe Calloway Story *(Prequel to the In the Arms of a Savage Series)*

When a Gangsta Loves a Good Girl

Caught Between My Husband and a Hustler

The Illest Taboo 1-2

To the Only Thug I'll Ever Love

A Lover's Heist: Chief and Gianna's Love Story

A Lover's Heist II: Rome and Lira's Love Story

A Lover's Heist III: Baby and Skai's Love Story

Crushed Velvet & Cashmere

Crushed Velvet & Cashmere 2

Entanglements

Never Had a Bad Boy Love Me So Good

Short Reads + Novellas:

Bi-Curious: An Erotic Tale

Bi-Curious 2: Tastes Like Candy

A Savage Calloway Christmas *(Christmas novella to the In the Arms of a Savage Series)*

Lovin' the Alpha of the Streets: A Valentine's Day Novella *(Valentine's Day novella to the Fallin' for the Alpha of the Streets Series)*

Awakened: A Paranormal Romance

As Long as You Stay Down

Solace in Seven

Solace II: The Final Cut

Something Bleu

Something Borrowed

Something New

The Knight Before Christmas: A Potomac Falls Short

I'll Be Home for Christmas: A Potomac Falls Short Book II

Triggered: A Potomac Falls Novella

Wasted Off You: A Friends to Lovers Novella

Because You Don't Know My Name: A Potomac Falls Novella

Will You Say My Name: A Potomac Falls Novella Book Two

Remember My Name: A Potomac Falls Novella Book Three

Every Thug Needs a Lady: A Lady and the Tramp Retelling

Ten Things I Hate About Lovin' You: An Enemies to Lovers Novella

In Exchange: An Urban Thriller

Children's Books:

Princess for Hire

Princess Twinkle Toes & the Missing Magic Sneakers

Little One, Change the World

Adjust Your Crown: A Self-Love Coloring Book for Children of Color

Non-Fiction:

Authors are a Business: The Booked & Busy Course Mini Book

BLP

Visit bit.ly/readBLP to join our mailing list for sneak peeks and release
day links!

Let's connect on social media!
Facebook - B. Love Publications
Twitter - @blovepub
Instagram - @blovepublications

**We hate errors, but we are human! If the B. Love team leaves any
grammatical errors behind, do us a kindness and send them to us
directly in an email to** blovepublications@gmail.com
with ERRORS as the subject line.

**As always, if you enjoyed this book, please leave a review on
Amazon/Goodreads, recommend it on social media and/or to a
friend, and mark it as READ on your Goodreads profile.**

By the Book with B Podcast: bit.ly/bythebookwithb